Requiem for a Dove

BY MARJORIE ECCLES

Requiem for a Dove
Death of a Good Woman
Cast a Cold Eye

(As Judith Bordill)
The Clouded Mirror
A Candle for Lydia

(As Jennifer Hyde)
Hill of the Caves
Handful of Shadows
Arabesque of Daisies
Winter Magic
A Secret Shore

Requiem for a Dove

MARJORIE ECCLES

A CRIME CLUB BOOK
DOUBLEDAY
New York   London   Toronto   Sydney   Auckland

A CRIME CLUB BOOK
PUBLISHED BY DOUBLEDAY
a division of Bantam Doubleday Dell Publishing Group, Inc.
666 Fifth Avenue, New York, New York 10103

DOUBLEDAY and the portrayal of a man
with a gun are trademarks of Doubleday,
a division of Bantam Doubleday Dell
Publishing Group, Inc.

Library of Congress Cataloging-in-Publication Data

Eccles, Marjorie.
    Requiem for a Dove / Marjorie Eccles. — 1st ed.
      p.   cm.
    "A Crime Club book."
    I. Title.
  PR6055.C33R47   1990
  823'.914—dc20   90-3180
                                      CIP

ISBN 0-385-41467-6
Copyright © 1990 by Marjorie Eccles
All Rights Reserved
Printed in the United States of America
November 1990
FIRST EDITION
RRD

Requiem for a Dove

Chapter one

Was it the woman herself, living self-contained and solitary, who had intrigued him so much, maybe because some awareness of the inescapable link between them, yet to be forged, was already with him? But he had no sense of that, then. It was only later that he came to feel that way. Perhaps it was simply the place.

A deep, narrow cutting through red rock, thickly wooded. Coins of light dancing on khaki-green water, still and sluggish between banks high with cow parsley and willow herb, and orange balsam bending to its own reflection. The towpath overgrown with elder and hawthorn and willow, dangerously undercut in places, bounded by the dark mouth of the tunnel entrance at one end and the first of the flight of three locks at the other.

Beyond the tunnel was the canal basin by the old gasworks and a flat grey wasteland of abandoned factories and warehouses; above the locks the industrial suburb of Holden Hill began. But here in this hidden valley, between a B road and the railway, the traffic noise baffled by trees, lay this place of silence and secrets.

The waterway, he'd learned, had been a branch constructed originally in Lavenstock's industrial heyday to bring sand up to the local glass factory, as well as iron ore for the foundries and coal for the gasworks, but no barge or narrowboat had passed within years along it. At this point the canal was choked with weeds and silted with mud; green slime covered the lock gates, though its upper reaches had been cleared by bands of volunteers and it was now navigable as far as the locks. There were plans to repair the flight and develop the section beyond the tunnel as a leisure area. Landscaping for that had already begun. Factories were being pulled down, warehouses had been converted into luxury flats and the basin into a marina connecting the canal with the Stockwell, which ran parallel with it for several miles in the valley.

It was this last which had led to Mayo's discovery of the place one day after he'd been inspecting one of the warehouse flats with a vague idea of buying, at a time when he'd over-optimistically had the idea that he might not always be living alone, and that one of the flats might not be beyond the means of a detective chief inspector. But although both hopes had been summarily dashed his irredeemably inquisitive nature—and even, he admitted with a grim wryness, a certain masochism—had led him on to explore the whole area further, pushing through the dank, echoing, bat-hung tunnel to emerge with surprised delight into a golden evening silence, tree-dappled and shot through with the iridescence of dragonflies.

He suspected few people used the canal at this particular spot. The absence of the usual detritus of rusty bicycle wheels and abandoned fridges, floating islands of indestructible polystyrene foam and old mattresses disfiguring the stretch beyond the tunnel was enough indication of this. The odd fisherman might occasionally manage to find somewhere to set up a stool and an umbrella, and an old rope dangling from a leaning sycamore led him to suppose unsupervised kids might lark about here from time to time. But he imagined the woman living in the old lock-keeper's house, at the point where the ground widened in front of the first lock, would be virtually undisturbed, left to the peace and the humming silence and the green water sliding soundlessly through the wooded clearing.

He realised he was seeing with temporarily enchanted eyes. In the dark winter days when there was no sun, or when mist rose from the canal like a miasma, it would be dismal. The dark little lockhouse wasn't convenient, being approached via a rutted lane with no easy access for vehicles. And yet—preoccupied with personal problems, walking along here several times lately in the hot dry spell that had come like a late redemption for a poor spring and summer—when he'd seen her sitting reading under the trees, or gardening, sometimes feeding her ducks, she had seemed apparently entirely contented and self-sufficient. She appeared so calm, so much a part of the place, shadowed and secret. A mythical figure almost, timeless, fixed in storyland . . . *"Once upon a time, there was an old woman who lived alone in her cottage with her six white ducks . . ."*

Only she wasn't old, not what you'd call old nowadays. A slim, nice-looking woman in her late fifties or early sixties, she'd raised her head when he passed, regarded him calmly with large grey eyes and then returned to whatever was occupying her. Apart from passing the time of day they'd never spoken.

Chapter two

Poised symbolically over the huge metal entrance arch into which DOVE'S GLASS was writ large were a pair of white marble doves, as artistically intertwined as if on some tomb of the Victorian era in which they had originated. More doves were engraved on the glass panels of the mahogany entrance doors to the offices, in case you might have missed the significance of the others. The carpet in Kenneth Dainty's large, old-fashioned but airy office was dove grey, though this may not have been intentional. Ken was not given to flights of fancy.

"Oh dear me, not at our best today, are we?" Mr. Bainbridge's ironic glance had followed Ken as he stalked through the outer office that morning with barely a nod to those present.

"Poor man, it's most likely Mrs. Ken on at him again over something."

"None of your business, Valerie!" Eyebrows lifted reprovingly over half-moon spectacles, his voice called her sharply to order. He was Ken's uncle by marriage, and the office manager, and therefore entitled to take occasional liberties, but she as Ken's secretary—and office typist and teamaker when the occasion demanded it—wasn't so privileged. In an office where everyone was known by their Christian names, he was never anything else but Mr. Bainbridge. He was painfully arthritic and went with a stick. He was due to retire shortly and should have gone years ago, but nobody had dared suggest it. In any case, no-one, including Ken, could imagine how the office would run without him.

"I'll bet it's true though," Val had retorted, unrepentant.

Ken was at that moment making a half-hearted attempt at dictating to her, with many *ums* and *ers* and constant second thoughts to interrupt the flow of her neat shorthand. She was a plump, cheerful girl who liked working for him because he

overlooked her tendency to misspell occasionally, largely because his own spelling was worse than hers, let her go promptly
at five-fifteen and gave her generous bonuses at Christmas. She
sighed now as ostentatiously as she dared and the unlikely object
of her sympathy, taking the hint, pulled himself together and
began to concentrate.

When he was finally through with his correspondence and
she'd gone away to deal with it, Ken left his desk and walked
heavily to the window where he stood, one hand braced against
the frame, the other thrust deep into the trouser pocket of his
well-tailored grey suit, staring without pleasure over a familiar
view that normally gave him a good deal of satisfaction. A powerful man with muscular shoulders and a short neck, with fresh-
coloured smoothly tanned skin and the curly forelock, rounded
forehead and wide nostrils of a handsome pedigree bull. A not
unattractive face, especially when people were doing what he
wanted, but just now set in a deep frown. What was he going to
do about Shirley's mother? What, for Christ's sake, *could* he do?
He'd spent most of last night lying awake worrying and was no
nearer a solution.

There must be one, somewhere. After nearly twenty-five
years with the firm, fifteen of them as an honorary member of
the Dove family through his marriage to Shirley and the last ten
as MD, virtually running the whole show—with Marion content
to let him do so—he wasn't going to allow her to ruin everything he'd built up, have it come crashing round his ears. What
daft whim had got into her, what in God's name did she think
she was playing at? He'd always considered her too deep for her
own good, too deep for him at any rate, though they usually got
on well enough, considering. But this latest thing, he raged,
staring moodily out, was beyond belief. It just wasn't on.

From this favourite vantage point at the window, with the
Stockwell valley spread out in front and descending gently towards Lavenstock, it was nearly possible to believe the sprawl
and workaday clatter of industrial Holden Hill, stretching down
and behind the factory, didn't exist. On this side of the slope,
where he could remember the last of the old nailers and
chainmakers and foundries standing cheek-by-jowl with corner
shops and the unlamented back-to-back houses of the sort in
which he'd been born, a private estate now stood, thrusting up

red gabled roofs through trees that had been planted and had matured over the thirty odd years of its existence. Gone were the other factories. Only Dove's remained, foursquare on the broad brow where it had been built 150 years ago, when old Enoch Dove had first trekked over here with his glassmaker's tools to set up on cheap land after a disastrous fire to his glasshouse in Stourbridge had almost ruined him. Here sons and grandsons and great-great-grandsons had continued in a small way their proud inherited Huguenot tradition of working glass until Wesley, the last and most ambitious of them, had died. After striving all his life to make the name of Dove synonymous throughout the world with elegant cut crystal and only partially succeeding, he had died a bitterly disappointed man, leaving only daughters, with no sons to carry on his name.

Shortly before Ken's marriage to Shirley, it had seemed to him that as a future son-in-law it couldn't do his prospects any harm at all to let it be known to Wesley that he was willing to change his own name to Dove, in the same spirit as the original Huguenots, founders of the family, had anglicised the French name of Douvre four hundred years ago. It was one of his few tactical mistakes. The old devil had soon silenced him with one of his sardonic looks and told him not to push his luck, and he hadn't made the suggestion again.

The canal flowed along behind the works before descending into the valley and where it curved gently in the distance some of the now converted warehouses by the old gasworks basin could be seen on their newly landscaped site. Because of the trees the flight of locks known as the Jubilee wasn't visible from here, but Ken could unerringly pinpoint the exact spot where his mother-in-law now lived. He would never understand why anyone with the money she had could actually choose to live in a hovel like that. And *ducks* for God's sake! She could have had a nice little bungalow with every mod. con. plus her own car— even someone to drive it if she'd wanted—but no. Not Marion.

Her obstinacy had been a source of mild irritation to him for years but Shirley, from whom in this at the very least he might have expected a bit of support, chose to defend her mother in this. "Oh, leave her alone, I've wasted enough breath trying to persuade her to get something better and it never does any good. Whatever people must think of me, I dread to imagine, but she never listens to my advice, so she certainly won't listen to yours. All she'll say is it suits her to live there better than living at The Mount.''

"Anything'd be better than rattling round in that damn great mausoleum!'' It stood there alongside the factory, unlived in but still fully furnished, the original inimical Victorian red-brick monstrosity built by the second Dove, shrouded in banks of rusty laurel and overgrown rhododendron. When old Wesley had died Marion had simply walked out and refused to go back, and for ten years she'd categorically refused to do anything about it. The doors would never since have been opened had Shirley not felt obliged to check things over occasionally, see the house was aired and arranged to have someone see to the garden every so often to keep the grass down. "But there's no need to jump off the other end of the bloody plank!''

"Must you be so coarse about everything?''

"I could be a lot coarser if I set my mind to it!''

She didn't laugh, as she would have done, once. She hadn't turned her nose up at a bit of rough in those days. But now, the local accent he'd never managed to get rid of, his mannerisms, his working-class relatives still living in the humbler parts of Lavenstock, she regularly had a go at them all. It was his good luck, he reckoned sardonically, that they'd met when she was so young, before she'd learned to be a snob, otherwise she'd never have looked at him, and he'd still be where he'd started, on the shop floor.

What was it that had turned her eagerness into restlessness and discontent? What—apart from that bit of bother she'd had nine years ago—had happened to the lovely, impulsive girl who couldn't wait for them to marry? he occasionally asked himself, though not consciously. He shied away from thinking about things like that, and not only because he wouldn't have wanted to face the answer. Leave such fancy thinking to people with more brains than he had, he told himself, people like Rachel. But sometimes, he couldn't help wondering.

At nineteen she'd been eager for life and experience, Shirley, too impatient to get on with it to waste, as she put it, three or four years at university, as her sister was all set to do. Okay, she'd done what she wanted, even to the extent of overriding the objections of the father she'd feared to Ken's own lowly status . . . she could find courage enough when she really must . . . but it hadn't stopped her from being bitterly envious of what she constantly and acidly referred to as Rachel's liberated lifestyle.

What did she want, for crying out loud? He spent his life trying to find ways of coping with Shirley, but he hadn't yet found the answer. In her own way she was as impossible as her mother was being over this latest thing.

Five to ten. His unproductive thoughts coming full circle were interrupted by Val buzzing to ask if he'd forgotten he was due to meet Jim Thorburn in the cutting shop at ten. "Okay, Val, I'm on my way."

He took the back steps, pausing on his way across the yard to glance in at the furnace hall and reassure himself that all was well, though he'd have been both surprised and annoyed if it hadn't been. He never could resist the pull that drew him there, however. Here was the heart and centre of the factory that was so intimate a part of him, where the raw, unpromising materials of sand and red lead and the broken and waste glass known as cullet were melted in the great domed furnace and the resulting glass metal spun into objects of astonishing and fragile beauty.

He stood inside the door, watching, his eyes growing accustomed to the darkness, the quiet broken only by a snatch of pop song from one of the youngsters, the tinkle of broken glass as a wineglass foot was cracked off a punty, the purring roar of the furnace. Traditionally it had been fired by cleft beechwood billets, later by coal, but now it was gas-fired, no longer dependent on the fickle direction of the wind or the reliability or otherwise of a stoker. From the rotunda of the furnace, the red eyes of the glory-holes glared out. Inside, the glass metal pulsated in the pots. The teams of men working it were stripped to the waist, sweat pouring as they dipped the long iron, spun and swung the fiery gather of glass and threw the iron with split-second timing from one to the other, with disciplined, organized, balletic movements. He remembered almost jealously how it was, he felt the old upsurge of pride, the sense of continuity, of belonging to a centuries' old tradition. He'd worked at the furnace himself, man and boy, rising to gaffer of one of the "chairs" working the glass, making objects shaped by his own will and sleight of hand, by the quick precision of his movements. He still got the itch to seize the blower's iron with its potentially dangerous orange-gold gather of molten glass, swing it, shape it with his breath, manipulate it and demonstrate his power to subdue the forces of gravity.

But he'd come a long way since his gaffer's days and his power was of a different kind now. He knew the business inside out, having started at fifteen as an apprentice glassblower, with marriage to the boss's daughter ten years later advancing him to managerial level. Some of his mates had looked askance at that but Wesley Dove had known what he was doing. He'd been a right old bastard but he didn't make mistakes about the men who worked for him. Ken had justified the faith put in him by revealing a flair for administration and a head for figures and with his practical experience and capacity for hard, untiring work, plus a certain ruthlessness, was soon master of every facet of the business. In the years since Wesley had died he'd increased the viability of Dove's Glass beyond all expectations.

And standing here at the hub of his universe, with all the world he knew and wanted around him, he felt a sudden access of resolution: he'd faced trickier situations than this one by far and got out of them. All it needed was a measure of concentrated thought until at last a plan of action would appear, plus a nimbleness of wit to foresee any difficulties that might arise, and the nerve to carry it through. His Taurean head lifted and he smiled. He was confident he had a good measure of all three.

Chapter three

Mayo would have had difficulty in believing the body was hers if it hadn't been for the spot where she was found. She'd been in the water too long and wasn't a pretty sight. Fish had already begun their nibbling at her water-sodden skin. Her tongue protruded horribly. She was wearing what had once been a navy and white silk shirtwaister and one smart white shoe, and her dark hair had come loose from its French pleat and streamed like Ophelia's. Her elegant pearl earbobs were still in place.

He looked down at what might once have been the woman who lived in the lockhouse and then put the polythene carefully back over the sodden body lying on the ground, breathing deeply. His stomach heaved as if this were his first corpse. God!

After all these years he thought he'd learned to control his physical reaction to the sight of a gruesomely dead body, though he was still moved every time to something like despair with the waste and futility of it. In this case it also affected him irrationally with a sense of personal affront, a shock of disbelief: this woman's life and his own had touched, however glancingly. What usually saved him from total despondency—and did so now—was the small, half-shamed yet undeniable frisson of professional excitement and yes, pleasure; such an end was after all a beginning for him, the unravelling of the threads to get at the centre of the knot. Or the start of the chase and the hunting down of the killer, depending on your terminology.

It was five to eight on a Tuesday morning early in September and although there had been a heavy dew it was already humming with heat, promising another scorcher. Mayo had only just arrived at the scene, thrown straight back into the thick of it the very day of his return from a fortnight's leave. He'd arrived at the station half an hour after the call had been received in the control room and when they'd told him a dead body had been found at the Jubilee Locks he'd driven over immediately, to find routine procedures already in motion.

"Everything under control, sir," DC Keith Farrar assured him officiously, as if he, and not Inspector George Atkins, tirelessly plodding his conscientious, unimaginative way towards retirement, was responsible.

Nevertheless, Mayo did a quick check round. A mortuary van was standing by with the other police cars, lights flashing, on the road above the rough track which led down to the canal, ready to take away the body after the police surgeon and the pathologist had examined it. The track itself had been sealed off by barriers. Two constables were marking off the area around her with yards of white tape, and Napier was busying himself with preliminary camera shots. Plain-clothes men and uniformed constables in shirt sleeves and helmets were grouping, ready to move in when instructed.

"Have we identified her yet?"

Mayo had swiftly regained command of himself and now asked the question routinely of Farrar, who despite the heat was looking his usual cool and uncreased self. He was an excellent young man of whom Mayo had high hopes, but who sometimes annoyed him with his too-obvious ambition, his determined keenness, his fancy dressing. Today he wore a crisp white shirt and light cotton trousers, his blond hair was smooth and unruffled. One day, thought Mayo sardonically, he'd forget and bring his tennis racquet with him as well.

The good-looking young detective constable hadn't failed to observe Mayo's pallor on seeing the body but was careful to keep his interest to himself. While acknowledging his superior's reputation, and conceding admiration, Farrar fully intended in time to surpass him and was therefore circumspect in his speech and actions.

"The man who found her says she's the woman who lives here in the lockhouse, sir, name of Dove, Mrs. Marion Dove. Sergeant Kite's taking a statement from him now."

Mayo nodded at this confirmation of what he'd already guessed.

"She was found in the pound, sir."

"The what?"

"The pound, that's what they call the bit below the locks, sir."

"Do they? Thank you, Farrar, for that information."

Mayo walked across to where Kite was sitting with an old man on a bench set underneath the window of the lockhouse, notepad on his knee, ballpoint in one hand and what looked suspiciously like the screwed-up wrapper of a Mars bar in the other. The lanky, perpetually hungry sergeant, like the rest, was in his shirt sleeves and sweating profusely. He stood up and greeted Mayo with his likeable, cheerful grin.

The old man's name, Mayo learned as he was introduced, was Percy Collis, a nimble old pensioner with a bright eye who had on a light blue buttoned cardigan and a peaked cotton cap that gave him the appearance of an elderly budgie.

"Terrible shock, summat like this, for an owd 'un like me," he greeted Mayo. "I'm eighty-six come next Thursday, yo' know."

Mayo dutifully expressed his surprise, put a few questions which launched the old man, who was nothing loth, into a repetition of what he'd already told Kite, of how he'd come across the body suspended in the reeds not far from the lock gates. He'd got over his initial shock, being too old for death to hold permanent terror for him, too experienced in human tragedy to be appalled for long, and by now he'd reached the point where he was beginning to enjoy his moment in the spotlight. Play his cards right and he might even get his name in the papers, you could see him thinking it.

"I come down the cut most days when the weather holds, see, for a bit o' fishing, like. There's a cunning old devil of a pike I've been after for weeks down yonder. Yo' hadn't used to be able to cotch a lot but it's better nowadays, they stop 'em turning out so much muck into the water." He paused, his glance travelling thoughtfully towards the sheeted bundle on the bank. He took another gulp from the beer bottle in his hand. "Reckon I might give it a miss for a bit, eh?"

Beside him on the ground by the seat lay his gear for the day, his picnic bag piled on top of his rods and lines, keep nets, collapsible stool and umbrella, his can of maggots. "Want a wet? There's another bottle," he offered Mayo generously. And with a nod towards Kite, "I've asked him but he don't want none."

"Keep it for yourself, Dad, bit early in the day for me," Kite said, and Mayo also shook his head.

"Suit yersels." Unoffended, the old man belched and eyed

Mayo. "Reckon her fell, then? Them steps is slippy sometimes. Only last week her sang out to me to watch how I come down."

Mayo had already made sure there were no obvious signs of anyone having slipped from the steep stairs at the side of the lock, though at the point where she'd been found the bank had broken away where someone might easily have accidentally missed their footing. Someone as familiar with those few yards of bank as the dead woman? In any case, he didn't think so.

The mud and debris of years had silted the canal up at the edges. Reeds and waterweeds with tough stems and flat, cabbage-like leaves had grown into it, making a thick, impenetrable mat, supporting the body just under the surface of the water.

"What made you so sure it was Mrs. Dove you found, Mr. Collis?"

"Who else could it ha' been? But it wor them ducks as made me wonder in the fust place. Gooing mad, poor little buggers, no food nor water in this heat and one on 'em already dead. Her wouldn't never've left 'em like that. When I rattled the door and give her a shout, no answer, so I knew summat was up and I started to have a good look round. I loosed the pen for a start— yo' should' ha' seen 'em goo!" Mayo glanced towards the canal and the five remaining ducks. Survivors, unconcernedly upending themselves into the water. "And then—then I come across her, poor wench."

"Known her a long time, have you?"

"Oh ar, ever since her wor a nipper. Come from Chapel Street her did, Bert and Flo Waldron's youngest. Her wed Wesley Dove, him what owned the glassworks, though he could've give her twenty year easy. Rolling in it, the miserable owd sod, and he couldn't even see her orright when he died! Her shouldn't've had no need to live poor like this."

The tone of voice wasn't unfamiliar to Mayo, evoking echoes of his own northern childhood, an environment with this same sense of tight community, where everybody knew everybody else and some did better than others, but good luck to them all the same. A good feeling of belonging, except that you couldn't blow your nose without everybody knowing. He asked Percy Collis how long Mrs. Dove had lived here.

"I'd be guessing if I said. Ten year? Dunno, rightly. Her used to mek me a cuppa tea now and again and I once asked her why her come here but her told me: 'I just like it quiet, Perce.' Well, it's all according, ain't it?"

"No accounting for tastes," Kite agreed. "What is it, Farrar?"

"Doc Ison's car's here, Sarge."

Mayo stood up. "Carry on with your statement to Sergeant Kite, Mr. Collis, if you don't mind, then we'll get a car to take you down to the station so it can be typed and you can sign it."

Percy Collis made no objections, signifying his willingness with a nod and another swig at the bottle, and Mayo followed Farrar down the path where he met the police doctor and Atkins at the foot of the steep stairs which descended from the first lock. "Morning, Doc."

The doctor acknowledged the greeting, his face grave. "This isn't what I expected, I must say."

"Expected?" Mayo looked sharply at the doctor.

"It's Marion Dove, isn't it?"

"You know her?"

Ison nodded briefly and knelt down on the grass beside the body. For what seemed like several minutes he stayed motionless, an unreadable expression on his face, then he said quietly, "Yes, it's Marion Dove, God rest her." He lifted the sodden left hand with its bleached and wrinkled skin, indicating where, across the back, ran a thick, ridgy scar, white as a worm. "Cut herself badly with a bread knife, years ago."

"Tell me about her, will you?" Mayo asked abruptly.

"I don't think I can tell you much. I've known her—and all the rest of her family—a long time, but only as patients. She's the widow of Wesley Dove—you know, Dove's Glass. There's a couple of daughters. The eldest's married to Ken Dainty, the chap who runs the works now."

"She'll have to be told. Where can we get hold of her?"

"They live out at Henchard, on the Ridgeway," volunteered Atkins, the fount of all local knowledge, naming the most prestigious road in Lavenstock's most affluent suburb.

Ison said, "Go carefully, she's inclined to be neurotic. I should try the works first, get hold of the husband and let him break it to her." He had shed his jacket and now began rolling up his sleeves preparatory to starting his examination. "All right, I'd better see what's what."

Mayo said, "You won't want me getting in the way. Tell them

to give me a shout when you've finished, will you? George, you come and give me a rundown on what's happened so far." He walked away, Atkins following like a faithful Saint Bernard. Mayo was a big man who carried himself well, but Atkins over-topped him. "Anybody been inside the house yet?"

"Had a quick look round myself. Nothing obvious. It wasn't locked, and the kitchen window'd been left open. Won't be told, will they?" The inspector shook his head sorrowfully. "A lot of money left in a drawer in the bedroom besides, but not touched seemingly. Her handbag's missing, though."

"How much? In the drawer?"

"Five hundred, at a guess. In tens and fives."

Mayo's eyebrows shot up. He told Atkins he would have a look round the cottage himself before Forensics arrived. "I'll come back to you."

"Right you are."

His long strides covered the distance back to the house and through the gate set in the low, dark-green painted fence which surrounded the garden. Kite and the old man had moved away. A short flagged path led from the gate to the front door, through a small plot bright with asters, pot marigold and nasturtium and fragrant with lad's love, with a Dorothy Perkins rambler and a honeysuckle either side of the door.

At the door the path divided and circled the lockhouse. Before going inside Mayo followed it round, shielding his eyes with his hands to peer through the windows. He got the general layout but could see little except that everything appeared to be in order, the kitchen tidy, the bed made. The building was one storey, rectangular, built of dark red Victorian brick. Its plan was simple. Just a front room with a kitchen behind it to one side of the central front door with one bedroom, and a bathroom made from what had probably once been a second bedroom on the opposite side. The cutting rose almost vertically behind the house and windows to the back had evidently been deemed unnecessary, those of the kitchen and bathroom being set in the side walls, the one overlooking a small vegetable garden with an abundant Cox's apple and a purple damson tree, the other the duckpen.

Amongst the vegetables a row of lettuces and a tomato plant in a growing bag, heavy with fruit, were flagging from lack of water. In the duckpen the dead duck lay with its head tucked under its wing, the water-trough was bone dry. How long could a duck survive without food or water? It sounded like a facetious riddle inside a Christmas cracker, but the answer might help to establish the time when their owner had died.

Pulling on protective gloves he opened the front door. His first impression was of darkness, though all the walls had been emulsioned in pastel colours to maximise the light. An open door showed him the bedroom, easily examined since it contained nothing except a single bed covered with a white hand-crocheted cotton spread, a chest of drawers with one top drawer locked and the money Atkins had mentioned in the other—all of five hundred pounds, yes—and why wasn't that in the locked drawer? He'd have that one opened as soon as Scenes of Crime had finished with it.

The wardrobe he found as he opened it housed a modest collection of unremarkable clothes. It looked as though she had been wearing her best when she died . . . the rest comprised the sort of garments he'd always seen her in: simple cotton dresses, blouses and skirts, a few sweaters and a mac with a detachable fur-fabric lining that would have doubled as a winter coat. The chest of drawers served as a bedside table and on it was a lamp, two half-full bottles of prescription pills and a thick volume of the *Complete Poems and Illustrations of William Blake,* inscribed in confident handwriting on the flyleaf, "To Mother, with love from Rachel." A Tesco checkout receipt for a modest £7.39 marked the place where a couple of lines were underscored in pencil: "He who kisses the joy as it flies, lives in Eternity's sunrise."

An unusual choice, Blake, not to everyone's taste by a long chalk. And whose choice, in this case? The mother's, or the daughter's? He flicked through it. Difficult poems some of them, well-nigh incomprehensible to him, the weird drawings and colour prints equally so. Visionary, said the accompanying text. Surrealist, he would have described them himself. The subject of one entitled *Pity* had a particularly unnerving effect on him. He *thought* it was a dead or dying young woman with a newborn child being taken up into heaven by a messenger on a winged horse, but whatever it was supposed to be the prone figure with streaming hair and hands clasped across her breast bore a shocking resemblance to the shrouded figure lying on the canal bank.

He closed the book abruptly and as he did so the supermarket receipt slipped out and fluttered to the floor. Bending to retrieve it, he saw there was something written on the back. In a very different handwriting to that inside the book's cover, small and slightly backward sloping, someone had written: "Steven, 10.30 Sunday." Before putting it in his wallet, he noted that the date was last Friday's, and slid it carefully into a small plastic envelope so that it could be tested later for traces.

The kitchen and bathroom were neat and orderly with nothing special to interest him. And very little in the tiny sitting room, except for a plain oak sideboard, the contents of which mildly surprised him. An Indian-style rug in front of the hearth stood on a floor of polished red brick, there were almond-green slubbed linen curtains and two armchairs slip-covered in flowered cretonne, and a low table upon which was set a chessboard with a game in progress. There was also a small bookcase which on inspection contained predominantly travel books and more volumes of poetry, mostly modern, with several library books on the top shelf of the same persuasion.

A simple home. Simple but not, as the old man had implied, poor. And through choice rather than necessity, Mayo was sure. Deliberate simplicity, almost to the point of anonymity. Marion Dove seemed to him to have pared down her life to all but essentials. No music, even. He, who found poetry difficult to understand and appreciate, but to whom life without music was unthinkable, had of course noticed at once that this hadn't been an obvious way in which her life was enriched.

Yet it was extraordinary what a peaceful atmosphere there was in this room. So strong as to be almost a force, as if the woman who had lived there had left her own attainment of it as an impression on the very air, so that he might pick it up. How much of this was due to the curious effect his own obsession with the place had on him? Mayo stood for a moment in the centre of the room, being very still, then went out of the house, closing the door behind him.

Chapter four

Ison was standing up, brushing the red sandy soil off the knees of his trousers. "That's it, then," he announced in typically brusque manner. "She didn't drown, she was strangled. Dead before she went into the water—though don't quote me. You'll have to wait for the PM to be certain."

The doctor's natural caution was always added to by his professional reluctance to commit himself, but Mayo knew him well enough by now to realise this practically amounted to a direct statement, and in any case the information came as little surprise to him. He'd seen enough bodies to have recognised the signs on this one and to have made a fairly accurate guess, even from his brief enough look at her, that someone had choked the life out of Marion Dove.

"Strangled, how?"

"Manually, by the look of the bruises on her neck . . . if she fought back, there's no other bruises to say so. They may of course find skin and tissue under her nails."

At least there'd be no dragging the canal, no rubbish tips to sift through, no waste ground to search for the murder weapon. Not when that had been someone's bare hands.

"Anything more?"

"I take it you mean when did she die? A couple of days, I'd say, three at the outside. Sorry, Gil, I know it's important to you to know, but it's not something I'm prepared to stick my neck out on at this point. Maybe Timpson-Ludgate will be able to be more precise at the autopsy, but I wouldn't count on it. You know as well as I do how difficult it is to tell. Find out when she had her last meal and we might be in a better position to say."

"Two to three days? That takes us back roughly to—Saturday, Sunday." Mayo thought for a while, then remembering what the doctor had said when he arrived, he asked, "What did you mean by saying this wasn't what you'd expected to find?"

Ison brought out a handkerchief to mop the perspiration from his brow and stared across the water, not answering immediately. A dabchick dived underwater with a plop, and a shaft of sunlight penetrating the canopy of leaves shone on a cluster of half-ripe elderberries, emerald bloomed with dusky purple. The scent of meadowsweet was strong, mingling with the dank, faintly rotten smell of the canal and the taint of corruption on the air.

"No," he said at last, "it wasn't what I anticipated. When I heard a woman had been fished out of the canal just here I automatically thought of Marion Dove, knowing she lived here. I expected to find she'd taken her own life."

"Suicide? Was she suffering from depression? Had she attempted it before?"

Ison said, "No, not clinical depression, that is. But she'd been having treatment for some time. She was suffering from non-operable cancer. She'd left it too late and I had to tell her a few weeks ago that her chances of surviving more than another month or so were so slim as to be non-existent."

"He who kisses the joy as it flies." Those underscored lines of poetry suddenly seemed unbearably poignant. A sense of fleeting melancholy assailed Mayo as he looked at Ison, shortish, bespectacled, middle-aged, tired. Of such stuff are heroes made. "It's a devil of a way to earn a living, Henry, yours."

Ison grunted, briskly rolling down his sleeves. "Yes, well, nobody ever made you become a policeman, either." Picking up his bag, he hesitated before leaving.

"Something bothering you?"

"No. No, not really." Ison frowned and ran a hand through what was left of his hair. "Just something niggling, but damned if I know what. Probably left the garage door unlocked or some such. Forget it."

He wasn't a man to be pressed and when he'd left, Mayo rejoined Atkins, who was standing with DC Deeley looking at the taped-off section at the edge of the canal where the bank had broken away. He looked around for Kite, found he had just sent old man Collis off to the station with Farrar, and beckoned him over. He then repeated what Ison had said for the benefit of the others.

"Poor woman," Kite said, and for a moment all of them were silent, subdued with the irony of life.

"Her handbag turned up yet?" Mayo asked Atkins.

"Not so far. After her attacker had got what he wanted, he probably chucked it in the bushes, or the canal. We'll drag for it, if necessary."

"She was mugged then, sir?" Deeley surprised them with the doubt evident in his voice.

"She was strangled, Pete, throttled," Kite pointed out patiently to the young DC. Deeley sometimes exasperated them all with his slowness, but he was showing promise and any initiative was to be encouraged. "Not knifed, or knocked to the ground, or clouted over the head. Deliberately strangled."

Deeley looked abashed, but unoffended. He was used to being put down. He accepted the fact that they couldn't all be smart alecks, like Farrar, but he knew he had his uses. He had hands like York hams, weighed fourteen stones. Put him in a punch-up and nobody had the edge on him, and though he was slow-thinking, he got there, in time. "She must have been going out, or coming back in, then," he said.

"Her door wasn't locked, nor the windows, and there was money in the house, so that seems unlikely."

"Then why did she have her handbag with her? She wouldn't take a handbag with her for a walk outside her own front door, sir, would she?"

He had a point, Mayo thought. Perhaps she had for some reason rushed out, handbag in hand, forgetting to lock up, and had been attacked. Why? Why had she rushed out, why had she been attacked? This didn't, he was thinking, have the appearance of an opportunist crime, a chance encounter on a dark night, a handbag snatch gone wrong, with death an unforeseen result of the attack. Yet if it had been a deliberately planned robbery, that implied someone with prior knowledge of something worth stealing, either in the house or on her person. Curious, then, considering the money in the drawer, and the unlocked house. "It doesn't make much sense. Anyone attacking with robbery in mind would have taken the opportunity of seeing what he could find in the house."

"Not if he panicked when he saw she was dead," Kite said.

"Fair enough. But don't let's get sold on the idea of this as a casual, unpremeditated attack."

"So if robbery wasn't the motive—" Kite let the rest of his sentence hang.

But Mayo was not, at this point, overly concerned with speculation about motives. "Then we're looking for something else, aren't we?" he said.

The pathologist, Timpson-Ludgate, in a great hurry and not as exuberantly cheerful as usual, thank God, had been and gone, promising to carry out the autopsy as quickly as possible, not adding anything material to Ison's findings. The body, sheeted in polythene, had been carried up the steep path to the mortuary van. Leaving Atkins to take care of what still had to be done at the scene, Mayo left with Kite to go back to Milford Road to put his superintendent, Howard Cherry, in the picture. Fortunately, on this occasion the station was within striking distance, near enough to make the setting up of a separate incident room unnecessary, a situation Mayo always avoided if possible. He always preferred to work from base, where all the investigating machinery—telephones, computers, transport, the rest—was already to hand.

"When I've seen Cherry I want you to come with me to see the daughter's husband—what's his name—Dainty, Kenneth Dainty," he told Kite as they followed the same path as the victim.

He wanted somebody with him at the first, all important interviews with the next of kin, another pair of perceptive ears and eyes, and there was nobody he'd rather have than Kite. Competent, tenacious and energetic under a sometimes regrettably flip exterior, despite his youthful, ingenuous appearance, he was an experienced detective and there wasn't much he missed. He had plenty of the same sort of drive that Mayo had, and they'd worked together long enough now to be on the same wavelength, so that there was the minimum of time wasted. Time which was a crucial factor in every murder investigation, before the trail went cold.

As they left the canal bank and began to walk up to the road, Kite said, "I'd nearly forgotten . . . have a good holiday, sir?"

His own, taken at the beginning of the school holidays with his wife Sheila and their two young sons, seemed a long way behind, and his tone was a bit wistful.

"Fair to middlin', thanks. Restful."

"Glad to hear it." Kite took the answer for what it was, true Yorkshire understatement. Circumspect as ever about his personal life, the DCI, but his holiday had evidently done him good. He looked fit and tanned, a lot more relaxed than he had for some time.

Kite's surmise was correct as it happened. Holidays weren't something Mayo relished these days. They never had been, truth to tell, even when Julie had been a little girl and Lynne was still alive and seaside or country holidays had been one of the great occasions of the year, like Christmas, planned months ahead. Now that he was alone and could please himself he generally managed to avoid taking the whole of his annual allotted leave. This time, however, he had felt the need for a break and had just spent ten days walking alone in the Western Highlands, staying at a small hotel which provided ample, wholesome food, plentiful hot water for luxurious baths when he returned tired out at the end of each day, and excellent malt whisky. It had only rained three or four times, he'd seen a golden eagle on the Isle of Eigg and he'd returned sunburned, full of well-being and rarin' to go.

During the long days tramping the hills alone, when he had met nothing that lived except for sheep and the occasional magnificent stag glimpsed dramatically on the skyline, he'd done a lot of thinking. Mainly about Alex and himself. He wasn't a man to go on bashing his head against a brick wall, he decided at last. What he needed was a strategy, and the strategy called for at the moment was to play a waiting game, to go along with the uncommitted relationship Alex wanted. Looking down from the height of a barren moor, ravished by the unexpected sight of a hidden loch between the hills mirroring the racing clouds of a blue sky, his mind blown clear and exhilarated with wind and sun and pure air, he'd suddenly been able to put things in perspective.

Alex was ambitious, sooner or later she would be off. She wouldn't stay a police sergeant for much longer. Whereas he, perhaps, had reached the desired limits of his own ambition—

for further promotion would mean a more and more desk-bound future, which was not where he was at. Maybe also she was wiser than he. Maybe it was only propinquity after his wife's death and his daughter leaving home to train for a career which had brought them together, and anything long term was not on. But this was travelling further than he was prepared to go at the moment.

"Kiss the joy as it flies." The words of the quotation came back to him. It was as good a philosophy as any.

There was a shout from one of the constables up by the lock gates. "Looks as though they've found it, the handbag," Kite said. But the constable was holding aloft the other white shoe.

They walked up the lane, small round stones slithering under their feet, and emerged on to the Compsall Road, where Kite stood looking round, his face registering utter incomprehension. "Why in God's name would *anyone* want to live here?"

The road bridged the canal at the top of the first lock and crossed a further stretch of industrial spoilation, long awaiting redevelopment. As so often hereabouts, topographical contrasts were marked. These desolate acres which signified the limits of Lavenstock's industrial area came to an end half a mile away at the Evening Lock, whereafter, like going through the gateway to another world, the canal wound lazily through a landscape in which cattle grazed in lush meadows, crops flourished and woods rose gently to the hills. But here was scrubby emergent grassland where the only signs of life were a few aged, moth-eaten donkeys and ponies looked after by some cranky woman. Almost treeless, bisected by the canal, bounded by Compsall Road. Along the roadside survived two or three scattered, tiny dark brick cottages of the sort that had been shoved up in a day and a night to establish squatters' rights during the last century, it was said. Holden Hill and its crowded factories and engineering shops veered off upwards to the right. Far to the left lay the remains of a forsaken brickworks, merely a blunt chimney now and some tumbledown walls. Further along was the Dog and Fox, a pub of unsavoury reputation.

Why live here? Looking round, Mayo couldn't argue with Kite's point of view; but below he had been vouchsafed a glimpse of Marion Dove's small secret world, and he thought he could understand.

He got into his car, then leaned out to speak to Kite. "By the way—those ducks. Get somebody to do something about them, see they're taken care of."

Kite looked blank. He knew nothing about ducks except that they tasted good with orange sauce. "Couldn't they be left to—er—take care of themselves? I mean, other ducks manage all right, don't they? Worms and things. Or have these forgotten how to forage for their own food?"

Mayo looked equally blank. "I haven't a clue. But see to it anyway." He grinned. "Or ask Farrar, he's sure to know."

Chapter five

Rachel was packing when Ken telephoned with the news.

"I can't believe it," she heard him say, from a long way off, it seemed. "The last time I saw her, on Saturday night . . . I can't believe it!"

What did he mean? She was too shaken for it to matter.

She was a sturdy, positive young woman with straight fair hair which she wore pushed behind her ears and clear hazel-green eyes under strongly marked brows. Decisions didn't normally present her with difficulties. Yet when Ken had at last rung off she sat where was was, unable to move, in a patch of sunlight that filtered through the Edwardian stained glass in the front door panels and dabbled her white cotton skirt with rich lozenges of colour. Gold, sapphire, blood red. Blood. But there would have been no blood, would there? Oh God.

She was quite steady. She wasn't shaking, there were no tears, just a hollow feeling of complete unreality. And coldness. How could she be cold in this stifling heat? Half an hour ago just the effort of putting her things into her case had been making the sweat run down her back.

Theory, she discovered, was of no use at all. In theory she was fully aware that she was in shock and knew what she ought to do about it. In reality she seemed to be totally incapable of even moving, simply overwhelmed by things which seemed complex beyond her power to do anything about.

Josh. Josh, she thought with release. Thank God, he would know exactly what to do. With stiff fingers she dialled. But when he answered she didn't know where to start. There seemed nothing to say except, baldly, "I can't go to Florence. My mother's dead." Somehow she managed to tell him how.

There followed the briefest of pauses. "I'll come over right away. Ten minutes."

And in fifteen, after a hard and steadying embrace and a foray into the kitchen to make a cup of strong, sweet tea, he was leaning his shoulders against the mantelpiece, a slight man with a clever, mobile face and horn-rimmed spectacles, watching her while she sipped.

"You go," she said, "there's no need to spoil the holiday for both of us."

"Go? Without you? The whole point of Florence was to show it to you, my darling. It'll wait until we can go together."

The endearment, which came as a slight shock, she recognised with mute gratefulness as a measure of his concern. Endearments weren't his usual style. That was more a matter of laconic amused tolerance which she at least knew masked a deeper sensitivity, plus a lack of pomposity and the sort of irreverent, ironic wit that made him popular with his students.

An art historian of some seriousness and distinction, with several well-received publications to his name, Josh Amory had so far managed to survive critical acclaim with modesty and humour. They'd met when she'd taken up her own appointment here as lecturer in the history department at the university three years ago and had been lovers for the last two. He'd never asked her directly to marry him, nor had they ever discussed the possibility in theory. She'd sometimes wondered whether this was from some reluctance of his own or whether it sprang from an innate delicacy which sensed without being told that she didn't want to share the life she'd made for herself, even with him. Their relationship was deep and tender, emotionally satisfying, but marriage was the final commitment and as far as she was concerned, one demanding total honesty. There were still areas of her life closed from him.

"You'll have to go to Lavenstock," he said.

"I suppose I shall."

"I'll drive you there."

"No!"

She was appalled at the strength and crudity of her denial and laid her hand on his to lessen the impact but if he was offended he gave no sign. "If that's what you want," was all he said, adding after a moment, "You're still cold, is there any brandy?"

"I think so."

Unruffled, as familiar with her flat as with his own, he went to the cupboard where she kept her drink, poured cognac and brought it back to her, moulding her fingers around the glass until he was sure she held it steady. His touch was firm and comforting.

Like her, Josh had been brought up to control his emotions, though for different reasons. His family, unlike hers, was impeccable upper class, a long line of distinguished soldiers with several brigadiers and a famous general adding lustre to his ancestry; public school and Cambridge had followed a sheltered childhood. Her own circumstances were undeniably more proletarian, grammar school and a redbrick university, because such wealth as her father had possessed hadn't persuaded him to expend it in the buying of privilege, either for himself or his daughters.

Diverse as their backgrounds were, however, it had never seemed to matter. What was important was their common ground here in the civilised and perhaps remote tranquility of this quiet, academic city. It wasn't any sort of inverted snobbery which made her want to keep the two strands of her life apart but simply that they were like two parallel railway lines, never converging, or only at some distant, illusory point. Here at Northumbria was fulfilment, shared assumptions and an intellectually stimulating, well ordered life. And there in Lavenstock were ghosts. Ghosts from the old house in Holden Hill—private ghosts, never far behind.

Something inside her shivered uncontrollably. She knew she had something of her father's darkness in her, something of her mother's hidden waywardness. It had always frightened her, now it threatened. There was always guilt somewhere when someone died, which had to be accepted and sooner or later be forgiven in oneself—she didn't fool herself that she was unique in that. If her mother had died from natural causes the remorse would still have been there—but now it had added to it the burden of anger. It was an obscenity that after all she had been through, and endured, Marion's life should have ended like this.

The anger was not new. Rachel had rarely, if ever, asked her mother for advice but rather been prone to give it, even from a very early age, and been annoyed and impatient when it was rejected. She'd always been so sure of herself, so certain that her rational way of thinking was right not only for her but for her mother. That last meeting for instance . . .

She told herself that she'd tried. But Marion had been adamant, gently stubborn and unyielding in the way only she knew how to be. It had driven her mad, she knew her mother's decision had been the wrong one, but how could you argue with someone in her position? She had by then had the answers to much of what had puzzled her in her mother's life, that she might have known before had she asked in the right way. She had spent the journey home bitterly regretting that she had never before paused long enough in her headlong pursuit of career and self-fulfilment to think it through.

She tried to remember what Ken had said, what he'd meant, but somehow it didn't seem to have registered. It was irrelevant anyway, what did it matter now? He ought to be concerning himself with how Shirley was going to take the news. Poor Shirley, in her expensive new house, so careful of her vowels and the friends she kept, with her own personal hang-ups. How much had she known about what had gone on in those dark years? Rachel imagined herself asking her sister but knew she'd never do so. Shirley would grow scarlet and uptight, and even if she'd known, she would never admit it. Not she, not Shirley. She would much prefer to pretend it had never happened.

But as the elder child, she must have known, thought Rachel. What else had contributed to that horrifying business nine, ten years—Michael was how old?—nine years ago. As it had contributed to Rachel's own attitude to marriage. They'd neither of them ever be free. It was a cycle, a vicious circle, spiralling from one generation to another.

Chapter six

Mayo kept his eyes on the back of Ken Dainty's dark red Volvo as the CID car followed it, weaving expertly through Lavenstock's twisting, busy streets, noisy with market day traffic. Kite drove. In the back sat WDC Rhoda Piper, a silent, stolid woman with red hair and a broad freckled face, who had remained in the car reading the *Guardian* while Kenneth Dainty was informed of the death of his mother-in-law, his brief telephone call to break the news to his wife's sister, and his later formal identification of Mrs. Dove's body at the mortuary.

Out towards Henchard, where the soil was red and the hills crowned with trees heavy with the heat of late summer, the harvest was in and the stubble fields, pale and golden, stretched either side of lanes becoming increasingly steep and narrow. Presently they were running along the elevated country road known as the Ridgeway bordering which, for about a mile, were architect-designed houses with landscaped gardens and sweeping panoramic views either side.

"Millionaire's Row," Kite commented laconically. Mayo grunted. There were some very showy houses along here, one of them occupied by a pop singer who had enjoyed a moment of fame, but in Mayo's opinion their reputation was exaggerated by the inflated prices they commanded when they were sold.

Dainty, driving his Volvo fast and surely, eventually made a stylish turn into a red tarmac drive which led up to a split-level house with low sloping roofs and picture windows. Though not as large as some of its neighbours, it was still a house making a statement about the prosperity of its owners. Either side of the drive shaven lawns swept down, with specimen trees strategically placed. Flowerbeds surrounded it in which were lavish displays of roses of every hue in their second flowering, unsullied by black spot or aphid. Even Rhoda Piper was moved to com-

ment on the perfume which almost overwhelmed them as they
alighted from the car and went to the door, where Dainty
waited for them.

"Oh, the roses!" He shrugged. "Yes, they do well round
here. Come in, will you?"

A short while before, Shirley Dainty had been staring round
her expensively furnished home, impatient and dissatisfied with
it.

The room itself in which she was standing was attractive, long
and low, with pine-clad walls and a ceiling-high fireplace in natural stone and a big picture window, but it somehow didn't look
as it ought, the overall effect jangled and she didn't know why.
It should have been perfect, everything in the room was new,
and colour-coordinated, and the draped silks and velvets of the
soft furnishings had looked so lovely in the department store
room display. Perhaps velvet and silk were wrong, maybe she
ought to have kept to the plain carpet, and not substituted the
brighter, patterned one. A shaft of sunlight caught the prisms of
the cut-glass chandelier and made her blink. The shiny new bro-
cade cushions she'd bought yesterday, punished into stiff dia-
mond shapes, marched along the length of the velvet settee, and
suddenly furious, she punched them into softer shapes, flung
herself down and lit another cigarette.

Why was nothing ever perfect? Why did everything, once so
earnestly desired, turn to dust and ashes once you'd got it?

Ten minutes later she was still sitting there, looking at the two
men and the woman who'd accompanied Ken into the room.
Detectives! She told herself she wasn't impressed with the chief
inspector, despite his size and those grey eyes that were watchful
and missed nothing. She reached out and lit another cigarette
and his eyes flickered. He didn't like to see a woman smoking;
she could always tell, but what was it to him? She tapped the ash
off impatiently. Ken began to speak.

She heard what he said and didn't believe it. Then she looked
at his face and saw that it was true. She felt her face crumple. She
put her cigarette in the ashtray and Ken put his arms round her
and for the first time in a long while there was, for a moment or
two, that old feeling of closeness and warmth.

Was there an easy way to communicate the appalling fact of murder? If so, Mayo wished he knew. They let her husband tell her and sat awkwardly by while he comforted her with a tenderness that sat oddly with his bullish appearance, his large hands gentle and a curious expression on his face as she allowed him to hold her head against his shoulder for a few minutes. Then her body gradually became more rigidly held away from him and presently she raised herself from his arms altogether and moved slightly along the sofa. Dainty sat up more slowly and stared fixedly through the window, his jaw set.

"It's not fair," his wife was moaning, echoing the uncomprehending and unanswerable lament of the bereaved everywhere. "She wasn't old, or helpless. She could have had a good twenty years in front of her."

So Shirley Dainty hadn't known about her mother's medical condition. For reasons of her own, Marion Dove had kept that to herself, and Mayo didn't feel it was up to him to add to her daughter's misery at the moment by informing her. She had cared for her mother, that was evident—unless she was a damned good actress. Her eyes were reddened with weeping, her mouth swollen, though the first genuine outburst of grief over, she was beginning to react with hostility and accusation, her tone if not her words suggesting to react with hostility and accusation, her tone if not her words suggesting she was almost as much outraged by the fact of her mother being murdered as saddened because she was dead. It was becoming ever more apparent that she was also deeply affronted by the manner of her dying, and alarmed at the thought of the unwelcome notoriety it would inevitably bring.

"It's disgraceful, this sort of thing—isn't it about time your people did something to stop it? Just what has to happen before one can be allowed to walk outside one's own home in peace without being mugged?"

"Forgive me, Mrs. Dainty, but it's by no means established your mother *was* mugged yet," he said gently.

"She was attacked, wasn't she? Her handbag's missing. What more do you want?"

"More facts at this juncture. But this has been a shock, very upsetting for you. We can come back later if you don't feel up to

it, though naturally we don't want to lose any more time than
we have to."

Dainty said quickly, "Would you rather they did, Shirley?"
He for one looked as though he'd be glad of a reprieve.

She shook her head and said she was all right. And despite her
nerviness, Mayo was sure she would be. There was no sign that
she was about to collapse or go into hysterics. Rhoda Piper
wasn't going to be needed for tea and sympathy. "What do you
want to know?"

Anything you can tell me about your mother, Mayo thought,
what sort of woman she was, what her relationships with other
people were . . . but knew instinctively she wasn't the person
to ask, even if the circumstances had been propitious. Everything would be subjective with her, everything judged by how it
affected her personally.

She was a good-looking woman, her bone structure excellent,
she had large hazel eyes and fine light brown hair that she constantly brushed back from her face, but she was too thin, at
thirty-five or so already on the way to becoming scrawny. Lines
of discontent pulled down the corners of her mouth and her
constant fidgeting—with her hair, her cigarettes, the fringe on
the armchair, her fingers with their long red nails twisting together—was beginning to get on his nerves. But there was a
dazed look behind her eyes that prompted him to be patient
with her.

"Thank you. It would help us if you could answer a few questions," he said, keeping to practicalities, "for instance, whether
your mother was in the habit of keeping large sums of money
about her?"

She stared blankly at him. "Cash? Good heavens, no! Who
does nowadays—it's all plastic money, isn't it? Not that my
mother bothered with credit cards. She paid what bills she had
by cheque and I know for a fact she never kept more than a few
pounds by her. But what difference would it have made if she
had? People are mugged for whatever can be got, aren't they?"

"We found five hundred pounds in a drawer in her bedroom."

"Five hundred pounds!" Her voice rose several tones. "But
that's not possible!" Astonishment silenced her, but only mo-

mentarily. "In the bedroom you say? Well, she was mugged outside, and whoever did it wasn't to know that, was he?"

He could appreciate her insistence on the mugging theory. It would be easier for everyone if that's how it turned out to be. The alternatives were undeniably more horrible. He wondered if they'd occurred to her.

As he began to question them about Saturday evening, which Mrs. Dove had apparently spent with them, the telephone rang in the hall. Mayo made a signal for WDC Piper to answer it and waited. He eased the hard cushion at his back. The room smelled aggressively of furniture polish and was an uneasy mixture of studied, conventional good taste and expensive, glitzy ostentation. That chandelier must have cost a couple of weeks' wages. It was as unlike her mother's home as it was possible to be. I know which I'd rather have, thought Mayo.

Rhoda came back. "Mrs. Dainty, it's your sister."

Shirley rose and walked quickly through the door Rhoda held open for her, and left open after she'd gone through. "Rachel? Oh, Rachel! Isn't it *awful?*"

Her voice was clearly audible to anyone at the other end of the room and since Rhoda was evidently obeying her instructions to keep her ears and eyes open and making a mental note of what she could hear, Mayo turned his attention to Dainty.

"Yes, as we've told you, she came over and had a meal with us on Saturday and spent the evening here. Most weeks she'd come over one of the days. Not Sundays, though. She nearly always spent Sunday with her sister."

"This week as well?"

"Presumably. She didn't specifically say so, but it was a fairly routine thing."

Kite made a note of the sister's name, and an address in Holden Hill.

"What time did she leave?"

"I drove her home at about twenty to eleven . . . later than usual, but we'd been watching an old Western and she wanted to see the end." He smiled faintly. "She dearly loved a Western."

"When you say 'home' I take it you mean right down to her door?"

"Have a heart, I've more respect for my suspension than that! I stopped at the top of the lane."

"And presumably walked with her down to the house?"

There was a small silence. "Well, no."

"No? There was no moon on Saturday night. It must have been very dark down by the canal."

"Look, I did try. We had the same argument every time I took her home. I always offered to go down to the door with her, but she'd never let me." The truculence in his tone, his bull-like appearance and the held-down energy that radiated from him didn't suggest a man so easily deflected. "She always said she knew the lane like the back of her hand and there was no need. She was a very independent lady, my mother-in-law."

All the same, thought Mayo, all the same. Who would let a woman go unescorted down a lonely lane late on a moonless night? Into the dark shadows, where on that particular night, a silent watcher might have been waiting? Perhaps Dainty hadn't. Perhaps he was lying and had in fact gone down with her, down that dark track. He was jumpy and anxious, not, Mayo suspected, telling the whole truth. He was big and forceful, though not especially tall, with powerful shoulders and broad hands, capable of great strength. Workman's hands, still scarred with old burn tissue from his trade but, Mayo had already noticed, with no recent, visible scratches. Dainty was an unfortunate name for one with his appearance to be saddled with, though Mayo guessed he'd probably long since ceased to be either amused or annoyed by jokes about it.

He tried a different tack. "Would you say you got on well with her?"

Dainty stood up and went across to a section of the wall unit that held drinks and held up a bottle, but when Mayo waved away the offer, he poured himself a stiff gin, barely diluted with tonic, drank it straight down and poured another. No doubt the horror of that mutilated body on the mortuary slab he had formally identified was still with him. No doubt he needed time to get his act together. Whatever the reason he was, under that brusque exterior, almost as tense as his wife. "She wasn't a person you could ever get close to," he said, coming back to his place on the settee, glass in hand. "But I think we understood one another."

Not a very satisfactory reply. The reply of a man who, despite the assurance and authority he'd shown at his office, seemed to need to tread warily in his own home.

His wife came back into the room. She'd been crying again, her handkerchief was a crumpled ball in her hand. She stood in the centre of the room and said, "She's coming down—she wanted to stay at the King's Arms to save bother but I said that was ridiculous, of course she couldn't." She looked hurriedly at her watch. "I shall have to make the spare bed up, get a meal—"

"Shirley, sit down. Rachel will have to take pot luck, she won't mind anyway."

"That's what she said, but that's not the way I look at it," she answered petulantly, but she resumed her seat, perching on the edge of the settee, obedient and surprised perhaps to an authority in him hitherto not apparent.

Mayo cleared his throat. "Had there been anything untoward, any trouble of any sort between Mrs. Dove and anyone lately? If there was anyone who didn't wish her well, we should know about it."

"If you'd known her, you wouldn't need to ask that," Dainty said. "She wasn't the sort to get involved in trouble, not Marion."

"Didn't wish her well?" Mrs. Dainty echoed, slightly contemptuous in a way Mayo didn't much like. "I suppose by that you mean did she have any enemies. Well of course not—she didn't have many friends, let alone enemies." She bit her lip. "What I mean is, she didn't socialise. She led a quiet life, she was a very private person, you might say a bit strait-laced. She didn't even smoke or drink."

After that put down of hers, he couldn't help but take pleasure in one of his own. "There was drink in her sideboard, half-full bottles of sherry, whisky, gin."

"Oh!" There was a split-second hesitation. "Oh, well of course that doesn't mean she didn't keep some to offer her guests."

And yet she had just said she didn't have many. There'd also been an empty gin bottle in the dustbin. Maybe Shirley Dainty didn't know her mother as well as she thought. He said, "A game of chess was set up inside the cottage. Who d'you think her partner might have been?"

She took her time before answering. "I suppose that must have been Paul."

"Who's Paul, then?"

"Paul Fish." The very faintest head toss was discernible as she told him that he was the grandson of her mother's eldest sister, now dead.

"How old is he?"

She shrugged. "Sixteen, seventeen? One loses track."

"And they played regularly?"

"Not regularly, but fairly often, I suppose. He was always down there, doing jobs for her, or that's what he used to claim. We all know why, of course. Why else would a young boy spend so much time with a woman her age? Out for what he could get, that's obvious, after she'd told him she'd see him all right in her will, wasn't he? Don't think, Inspector," she added sharply, her colour heightened, "that my mother lived down there in Jubilee Cottage because she couldn't *afford* anything else. She wasn't a pauper, far from it! Besides which, she had The Mount, the family house on Holden Hill to live in if she'd chosen to."

"I think I know it—a big house for one person living alone, if it's the one I'm thinking of. Next door to the glassworks, isn't it?" Mayo asked, interested in her terminology. How much more upmarket "Jubilee Cottage" sounded than "the lockhouse"! "Who lives there now?"

"Nobody." It was Dainty who answered. "She refused to sell it or even to get rid of the furniture, though we're chronically short of space at the works, and we could at least have used it for offices." His tone was resentful, but the thought occurred to Mayo, and must at the same time have occurred to Dainty, because he attempted to shrug off what he'd said with a rueful gesture, that now there was nothing preventing it.

Mayo had come across many motives for murder and learned to discount nothing, though he thought it rather fanciful to imagine Dainty might have killed his mother-in-law for more office space. And yet—a quarrel on the subject, tempers raised . . . But he thought Dainty a very self-controlled man, and by no means a fool, who didn't easily lose his temper. He might, on the other hand, very well be the sort to nurse a grudge.

"I'd like to have a look around The Mount, if I may."

Shirley Dainty threw him the incredulous sort of look he

might have received if he'd asked permission to wander around Buckingham Palace, but Dainty seemed unconcerned. "If you wish. One of us will go with you."

"That won't be necessary. If you could just let me have a key. I'll give you a receipt for it, of course."

He could see Mrs. Dainty welcomed this request even less, but he held out his hand and while she unwillingly fished a key ring from her handbag and began to work a large mortice lock key from it, he took the supermarket receipt from his wallet and asked if she recognised the handwriting on it.

She handed over the key and looked at the back of the receipt, still in its plastic envelope and confirmed that it was her mother's. A tiny pause. "Steven? Who's that?"

"I was hoping you might know."

He kept his eyes on the two of them and there was no response. But as sure as God made little apples, one of them knew. Which one, he couldn't tell, maybe both, but the enquiry had prompted a frisson of recognition—alarm—fear—emanating from someone in that room.

"What time did you go to bed on Saturday night, Mrs. Dainty?" he asked.

"About ten minutes after I'd said goodnight to my mother, it would be. I emptied the dishwasher and set the breakfast things out because we were playing golf the next morning and had an early start. Then I went to bed. Oh yes, I also stacked some leftovers in the fridge, so it might have been a few minutes more."

"What did you have for dinner?" he asked, apparently idly.

"A *ragout* of beef with courgettes and potatoes *Lyonnaise, tarte aux pommes Normandie,* coffee and biscuits to follow," she pronounced immediately, without batting an eyelid.

"And garlic," said Dainty.

His wife pointedly ignored this. "Why?" she asked Mayo. "Why do you want to know that?"

He thought it best not to enlighten her. Relatives were apt to get upset at the thought of what went on at post-mortems. Instead, he said, "A heavy meal like that, you must have slept well."

"Yes, but then, I always do because I take a sleeping tablet, otherwise I'd never sleep at all."

"So you wouldn't hear what time your husband came in?"

"As a matter of fact, I did. I hadn't quite dropped off, and I looked at the clock when I heard the door. It had just gone eleven. Now look, if you've finished, I have to get ready for my sister coming—"

"We'll just go through Sunday, if you don't mind," he said, unmoved. She made an irritable gesture and sat impatiently while he found out how they'd spent the day . . . golf in the morning, drinks and a snack at the clubhouse, home and a snooze with the Sunday papers, then out to dinner with friends.

"Well, that's it for now," he said at last, standing. "Unless my sergeant has anything to ask."

Kite looked over the notes he'd taken and shook his head. Rhoda coughed, and looked at Mayo. He nodded. She asked, "Do you remember what your mother was wearing on Saturday night, Mrs. Dainty?"

"Of course." There was a split-second hesitation. "She had her Liberty print skirt on, with a cream silk shirt and a caramel-coloured cardigan."

"Thank you."

"He'll have to come up with a better story than that, otherwise he won't be getting *ragout* of beef and *tarte aux pommes* where he's going," Kite said.

"Oh, I don't know," Rhoda offered, with unexpected humor. "Except they call it beef stew and apple pie in there."

Mayo grinned, then complimented her on the question about Mrs. Dove's clothes, causing her to flush, though not very becomingly, with her red hair. "And since she wasn't wearing what Mrs. Dainty described when she was found—"

"Maybe we're meant to assume she wasn't murdered until Sunday? You think she's covering up for Dainty, then, sir?" Kite asked. "Though they weren't exactly lovey-dovey, were they?"

"That doesn't mean a thing," Rhoda answered, encouraged out of her usual taciturnity.

"We're jumping the gun a bit, anyway, aren't we, assuming that he did it?" Mayo said, but he said it absently. He was half thinking on the same lines as Kite, that at the moment it did seem that Dainty was the most likely suspect, and that the obvious one was usually the right one. It looked as though he'd had the opportunity, he was certainly physically capable of it, and probably, if Mrs. Dove had been as wealthy as her daughter implied, he might well have had a strong motive.

But the other half of his mind had been thinking that there had been something odd about Mrs. Dainty's reception of the news. She might well indeed, despite appearances to the contrary, be worried for her husband, or trying to cover up for him, but he'd be very interested to know why also, deep under the layers of shock or grief or affront, or whatever other emotion she'd shown, she was also personally very much afraid.

Chapter seven

It had turned up in the water at the very edge of the canal, down in the reeds where the body had been found and that, unless it had indeed been a mugging gone wrong, disposed of Mrs. Dainty's favourite theory, because the contents of the handbag were apparently intact. It seemed probable that it had fallen in while she was being attacked, rather than having been tossed away. It was a shoulder-type, of soft navy-blue leather and now that the canal mud and slime had been cleared off, was seen to be of excellent quality, though well worn. In it were: a purse containing just over twenty-four pounds in notes and coins, a cheque-book and an appointments diary in a leather wallet, a comb and a compact, one crumpled lace-edged handkerchief and one folded one, a pair of spectacles in a case and a small bunch of keys, one of them presumably the key to the locked drawer. But that had already been opened, and found to contain, apart from predictable personal papers such as insurances, bank statements and bank books showing appreciable balances, only some old photographs of her children, a lock of baby hair curled into a piece of tissue paper, and two pairs of baby shoes.

Kite regarded with an appraising eye the contents of the bag spread out on a table in the corner of Mayo's office. "A lot less than most women cart around with them," he remarked. "You need a forklift truck to pick Sheila's bag up."

But it was what Mayo was coming to expect of Marion Dove. Neat, sparing, nothing unnecessary. Even the things found in the drawer, a mother's usual sentimental trivia, had been few. He picked up the cheque-book, which had been inside the leather wallet and now that it had been dried out was reasonably legible. There were only two blank cheques left of the original thirty. Mayo examined the counterfoils at the front of the book and after studying it for a while handed it to Kite.

"Take a look at this. What does it say to you?"

Kite said presently, "Fairly obvious, isn't it, if you look at those bank statements as well. Why else would she draw all these large amounts out? It's a fair bet she was being blackmailed. Very interesting."

"Interesting, but not conclusive. It's more often the blackmailer who gets the chop, rather than the victim."

"Unless she refused to pay."

"The last withdrawal was on Friday. A thousand pounds drawn out in cash—and only five hundred of it's missing," Mayo pointed out.

"Perhaps she was paying in five-hundred-pound instalments."

"Not as a regular thing. Not according to the statements. She's been drawing a lot of money out, but not regular amounts, or at regular intervals. But if it wasn't blackmail money, I'd very much like to know what she *was* doing with it."

The sister's house turned out to be small and brick-built, in a long terrace of similar houses, whose front doors opened straight off one of the sloping back streets of Holden Hill. She was smartly got up in a silk blouse and tailored skirt, a plump and robust woman with careful make-up whose hair had been streaked and touched up back to the warm blonde it must once have been. Looking a sprightly fifty-four rather than the sixty-four he knew she was. Not very like her sister, Mayo guessed, and rough-edged but good as gold. A mouth that looked as though in normal circumstances it would smile easily.

"Cuppa?" The invitation was issued as soon as they stepped into a tiny hallway at the foot of a steep flight of stairs. Thanking Kite for the post he'd picked up off the mat, remarking that it seemed to arrive at any time these days, Mrs. Bainbridge manoeuvred them from the hallway into a small, cheerful front room where a tray was set out on the coffee table.

"Please don't go to any bother."

"A cup of tea's no bother to me. Don't know what I'd do without it."

"In that case, thank you, it would be very welcome."

The kettle, she assured them, was already on the boil. With instructions to make themselves comfortable, she left them while she went out to the kitchen.

Mayo used the opportunity to take in the sort of details his policeman's training had taught him to observe: the shining bay window, curtained in crisp, spotless net shaped to rise above the sill at the centre though not, it seemed to let in more light, for in the space thus provided stood a large and healthy sansevieria, its leaves as glossy and polished as everything else in the room. The three-piece suite, one with the exaggerated wings and splayed legs of the 1950s, worn and shabby on the arms, standing on a carpet with a pattern of the same vintage that was wearing threadbare. A gas fire fixed into a tiled surround, with framed photographs set out on the mantel.

Mayo bent to study them. At one end was a pretty, laughing girl with a firm rounded chin, wearing the WAAF uniform of the last war, recognizably Gwen Bainbridge. At the other a distinctively good-looking young flight-sergeant sporting the one white flash of an airgunner above the breast pocket and grinning at the camera with the youthful certainty of immortality. In the middle, in the place of honour, was their wedding photograph. He in uniform, she in white with a veil, the bridesmaids flower-wreathed and long-skirted . . . even in wartime it had been managed somehow, dried fruit for the wedding cake and clothing coupons garnered from far and near. There were two bridesmaids, neither of which Mayo could identify as her sister Marion.

"I see you're looking at my photos, Robert and me," remarked Mrs. Bainbridge, returning with the teapot under a cosy in one hand and a plate of biscuits in the other.

Mayo suddenly made the connection. Robert Bainbridge? Wasn't that the name of the office manager who'd received them at Dainty's office that morning? It took an act of will to relate that precisely spoken, painfully moving, bloodless little man with this dashing rear-gunner, but substitute a bald dome for that abundant dark hair, add a pair of gold-rimmed specs and forty-odd years and it could be done. Even possible, then, to partner him with this woman. Gwen Bainbridge in her prime must have been quite a girl. She wasn't bad now. Nice-looking legs, her feet shapely in high-heeled shoes. Good skin still, carefully made up. He liked the courage of that. She was putting a brave face on it and what it was costing her was showing only in the misery in her eyes and the exaggerated steadiness with which she poured tea into generous-sized mugs. "You won't want teacups, that right?" she announced, rather than asked, in a matter-of-fact way.

"Right, missis," Kite assured her colloquially, as comfortably at home with her as with his Auntie May up Mapleton Street and striking exactly the right note, Mayo was pleased to see, as Mrs. Bainbridge's rigid grip on the teapot handle relaxed and she gave him a glance that was very nearly a smile. "Three sugars, please."

The offer of a little drop of something in the tea having been refused, she shrugged and sloshed a generous amount into her own before handing out the biscuits. "Go on, they're ginger, fresh-baked . . . gave me something to do, it did. They insisted at the shop I have the rest of the week off, but I wish they hadn't. I'm that lost already . . ."

She was suddenly too choked with emotion to go on. "Oh God, I'm sorry," she managed after a moment, blinking and pulling out her handkerchief. "I can't hardly get used to it, yet."

"Don't apologize, Mrs. Bainbridge—I'm only sorry to have to face you with questioning at a time like this—" Mayo began.

She tucked the handkerchief away, reached out for her mug and took a big gulp of tea. "That's all right, m'duck, you have your job to do. Don't take no notice of me, I'm all right, now. It just keeps coming over me, that's all. Ask me anything you want —anything that'll help catch him that did it."

As she gradually relaxed with the help of the whisky-laced tea, she became talkative. Talking was a natural state with her, Mayo guessed. Bit of a rattle-pate probably, but all the better, from his point of view, the more garrulous the better. They quickly learned that she was employed part-time at Betty's, the small dress shop down Holden Hill Road where she'd worked for over twenty years. It was a nice little job, she got her clothes at discount (which explained her smart and up-to-date appearance, Mayo thought) and she wouldn't deny that every little helped. Maybe she'd give it up when her husband retired next year, but she'd miss it, though not as much as Robert would miss working for Dove's. They thought a lot about him up there, Ken Dainty was always saying he'd be hard put to it to find anybody else who could run the office like he did. She fetched up a deep sigh. "He should have finished long since, but he can't abide not being occupied. Which is all very well, but look where it gets him—laid up in bed half the weekend! But he won't be said, nothing'll stop him if he's determined. He makes me that mad sometimes." She said it as though she loved him. Her face shone as she spoke of him.

So it was as Mayo had thought—he *was* the same Bainbridge. Well, we all have our moments of glory, all are golden lads and lasses come to dust.

"It's in his spine, you know, trouble from his old war wounds, or so they say. He was shot down just after we were married and never been right since. It's hard, though, watching him go downhill. They gave him a DFC for bravery, but that's not a lot of compensation, is it?"

It was obvious that like many childless women, she lavished all the warmth and love of which she was capable on her husband. Mayo guessed she would face the prospect, bleak enough for both of them, with as much fortitude as she attributed to her husband.

She said abruptly, "Who could have hated her enough to kill her like that? She wouldn't have hurt a fly, our Marion." It was a universal comment Mayo had learned as a rule to take with a pinch of salt, though it was always possible this might be one of the exceptions. He asked Mrs. Bainbridge when she'd last seen her sister.

"Friday afternoon. She stepped into the shop for a few minutes."

"Not later than that? Didn't she come to you as a regular arrangement on Sundays for lunch?"

"Not this Sunday she didn't. She usually came about half past twelve, left home at quarter past. We waited for her till half past one, then I gave her a ring but there was no reply so we gave it up as a bad job and carried on without her. I had a nice shoulder of pork and there wasn't no point in letting good food spoil and dry up."

Kite's pen was busy noting the times. If she had been dead by then, and assuming all parties were telling the truth, if Ken Dainty had last seen her about ten-forty the previous evening, this narrowed the length of time during which she could have been killed to about twelve hours. "Weren't you worried when she didn't turn up?" he asked.

"Not specially. Mad, more like, that she hadn't bothered to let me know." She hesitated. "To tell you the truth . . . we'd had a few words."

Another revivifying gulp of tea helped her to go on. Mayo picked up his own mug and took a scalding sip. It was strong enough to strip paint.

"Look, she was my *sister,* we could have a difference of opinion and not let it rankle after. I just expected she'd turn up as usual for her dinner, we'd both say we were sorry and that'd be the end of it. When she didn't I thought she'd taken the huff, though that wasn't like our Marion at all. I reckoned I'd give it a couple of days and then go down and see her and smooth things over. And now it's too late." She pushed biscuit crumbs around her plate with her forefinger. "Our mum used to say, 'Never let the sun go down on your disagreements.' She was right, wasn't she?"

The terrible thing about death was that it brought out all the old hackneyed sentiments, and it wasn't any less irritating when many of them turned out to be truisms, Mayo reflected, but she was welcome to them. Comfort came in all guises.

He said gently, "Could I ask you what it was you'd disagreed about?"

"You could, but I'm not going to tell you," she answered decisively, rallying with some spirit. "It's got nothing to do with what's happened."

When it came to murder, in fact, Mayo regarded nothing as too irrelevant to consider, but she'd closed her lips firmly and he had to accept he would get nothing by pressing her. He took another cautious sip of the tea which seemed to have acted on her like a shot in the arm, then put the mug firmly back on the tray, declining to have it topped up. If Mrs. Bainbridge could drink that, especially laced with whisky, she was a braver man than he. He made a better bargain by taking one of the only two biscuits Kite had left.

"I'll tell you something, though," she said abruptly. "I don't know what it was, but she was different lately. It wasn't anything I could put my finger on, know what I mean? But she'd lost a lot of weight and if it hadn't been that in a funny sort of way she somehow seemed happier than she had for years, I'd have thought she had something the matter with her—you know, that she was poorly. She'd had a few days in hospital for observation a couple of months since and I did ask her, but she said everything was all right . . ." Her voice trailed off as she felt the silence. "Oh God, there *was* something, wasn't there?"

Her glance travelled from one face to the other. She needed no answer. "Cancer, was it? Was that it?"

"I believe so. But according to Doctor Ison, if that's any consolation, she couldn't have lived long in any case, Mrs. Bainbridge."

At that she turned on him with unexpected fury. "Oh, so that makes it all right, does it? She'd outlived her usefulness anyway so it doesn't matter she was got rid of and thrown into the cut like a piece of old rubbish?"

"Now Mrs. Bainbridge," Kite began.

"All right, I shouldn't have said that, it wasn't called for—but she'd a right to what was left of her life, hadn't she? I just wish I'd known, that's all. I wish I'd known."

There were no tears now, but the silence was heavy. Mayo gave her time to collect herself. She struggled for composure and presently she was able to speak. "I shouldn't really be surprised she didn't tell me, she was always a bit secretive, you never knew what she was thinking. She was the clever one, got a scholarship to the High School, and all. Not like me, I never could add two and two together. Her teachers wanted her to go on to university, but . . . well, anyway. 'What's it matter, where's it going to get you, all that reading and swotting?' I used to say to her. 'Take life as it comes . . . have a good time while you can.' No use talking to her, though. She could be stubborn, and she'd just go on in her own quiet way, doing what she wanted."

She underestimated herself, Gwen Bainbridge. Not a clever woman maybe, not in the same way she said her sister had been, but not lacking in commonsense and shrewdness.

"It paid off though, didn't it?" he suggested. "Mr. Dainty's told us she ended up owning Dove's glassworks."

"Well, if you mean it paid off for her to marry her boss, then it did. She was Wesley Dove's secretary before she married him, that's how she came by all that. Twenty-five she was to his fifty-one, and that never seems right to me, big difference like that. Everybody thought she'd done it for his money, but it wasn't that, she was never interested in money. Though of course," she added wryly, "that's easy when you have plenty, isn't it?"

Did he detect the shade of an old envy, perhaps unrecognized, almost certainly never admitted, but never quite exorcised? It would be understandable. It seemed self-evident that there was little spare money to throw around in the Bainbridge household.

"God knows why she did marry him, but she was a good wife to him, and she was entitled to a bit more than she got. He was, excuse me, a bastard, and living with him was no bed of roses, to put it mildly."

"They weren't happy?"

"Happy?" Her laugh wasn't amused. "God, that house—The Mount—used to give me the creeps every time I went in. It takes some crediting, but it's gospel truth—he wouldn't have a stick nor a stone changed, every blessed thing was just as his mother had left it—and his grandmother and all, I shouldn't wonder. You should have seen that cooker—and as for the bathroom, well! How she stuck it, I'll never know. No wonder she got out as fast as she could when he died."

"Is that when she went to live down in the lockhouse?"

"That's right. They didn't want her to live there—Shirley didn't, anyway, not good enough in her opinion—but it wasn't a bad little place. Better than the one in Chapel Street where we lived when we were kids I can tell you. That got a bomb on it during the war and good riddance. It was what she chose, the lockhouse, it was quiet, but she wasn't lonely. She wasn't a what-you-call-it, a recluse, you know, she was always happy with her own company, just dreamy, romantic like. Anyway, I used to pop down to see her a fair bit, she came up here every Sunday and Shirley would ask her up to that posh house at Henchard for a meal—when they didn't have company, that is." She added drily, and with a sharp look that said a lot, "They'll come in for a fair bit, you know, her two girls. She's left The Mount to the pair of them, and money besides. I expect they'll be selling up—there's stuff in there worth a mint, whatever my opinion of it. It's thought a lot of nowadays, they tell me. Shirley won't be able to get her hands on it fast enough—she's greedy, that one, always was. Grab, grab. Hopeless, she is. Lives on her nerves."

She checked herself sharply, whatever else she'd been going to say—and there had been something—was left unsaid.

Mayo saw wisdom in not replying to derogatory remarks about one of the family. He was beginning to have a hunch that there was no need to look for an alien element in this murder, that whatever had occurred to cause the death of Marion Dove had its roots within the intricate web of family relationships. And such close-knit entities might be at daggers drawn among themselves but let any interloper or outsider, any comer-in as he was known hereabouts, dare to interfere or criticize or want to know why and they would rise as one against him. He'd had to conduct other similar enquiries on countless other occasions and the prospect of doing so again didn't fill him with unalloyed pleasure.

"You understand in a case like this it's necessary to check on the movements of everyone close to Mrs. Dove," he said. "So what about Saturday evening, what did you do then—and what about Sunday?"

"It wasn't what you'd call a cheerful weekend, what with Robert being so bad and all. I stayed in Sunday afternoon watching telly while he went up to rest, but I popped out both Saturday and Sunday night to help out in the bar at the Fighting Cocks—I do occasionally when they're short handed, it's a bit extra. I wasn't keen on leaving Robert, him feeling so poorly, but I'd promised and I didn't like to let them down, and there wasn't anything I could do for him after I'd given him his pills. I left as soon as they closed, and I was home both nights before quarter to eleven."

Kite looked up from his notes. "That was good going, from the Fighting Cocks."

"I didn't walk—least, I walked there but I was driven home. We don't use the car a lot. It's on its last legs, I'm no driver and Robert can't manage it now. That nice Valerie from the office gives Robert a lift to and from work, so we let a young relative of ours use the car on condition he pays for his own petrol and runs me about now and again when I need it."

"What's his name?"

"Paul Fish. He's the grandson of my sister Beattie that died, her daughter Norma's son."

A shade of reserve had crept into her voice as she gave the

information. Kite wrote the address down. Wasn't that the young man who used to play chess with her sister? he asked.

"How d'you know that?"

Mayo told her about the chessboard which had been set up, and what the Daintys' had told him about Paul playing with Marion. "Nice of him to bother," he added, "not every lad his age would."

"That's right." Her face softened. "But Paul's like that. Marion thought the world of him. He'd run errands for her and keep things fixed up for her, he's handy that way. He does the same for us, we've always made him welcome here, and so did she. Here, you're not thinking he had anything to do with it, for heaven's sake? Not Paul, never! He's still at school, he's only just gone seventeen!"

Mayo thought, since when had being seventeen been a bar to violence, theft, rape, murder or any other crime that could be thought of? But no, he told her, they'd no reason at all to suppose Paul was involved in the murder at the moment, but as they weren't in a position to know yet who might have information that would help, they needed to talk to everybody who'd seen her recently, and that included Paul.

"Well, God help you if Charlie Fish's around when you do."

"His father? Likely to cause bother, is he?"

She hesitated, then closed her lips firmly. "Better not say, I've been in too much hot water as it is for interfering in that direction. You'll find out for yourself. But go easy. There's been enough trouble down there."

"Wonder why they're so hard up?" Mayo remarked as they drove off, thinking about the worn carpet, the shabby, dated furniture, the references to needing money.

"That's what I was thinking, but did you see that big envelope in the post?" Kite asked. "It was from Tixall's, in Sheep Street."

"The estate agents?"

"Right. Think how much more convenient a bungalow would be than that house. Not one for anybody who finds it hard to get about, is it? Those stairs, for one thing! What I thought was, if he's due to retire, they've likely been thinking of moving and they've been pulling in their horns a bit—you need all your resources these days, property the price it is . . ."

"You know, I think you're probably right, Martin. So a nice little nest egg from her sister isn't going to come amiss. They seemed close, it'd be funny if she hadn't left her anything." Thinking on those lines, it occurred to him that it was time he made contact with Mrs. Dove's solicitor. From the size of those bank balances alone, never mind what else she owned, somebody was going to be appreciably better off, and he'd very much like to know who.

Chapter eight

In the event, he was saved from the trouble of doing so by a telephone call immediately following on Kite's departure from the station to catch Paul Fish on his arrival home from the comprehensive school. It was from Deeley, who had been left on duty down at the Jubilee Locks, a stolid and immovable presence to repel the inevitable ghoulish onlookers drawn to the scene like iron filings to a magnet whenever word got around that a murder might have taken place.

"The phone in the house here rang a few minutes ago, sir— Mr. Crytch, the solicitor it was, ringing Mrs. Dove. He hadn't heard the news about her and he's on his way to see you, sir, says he'll be with you in a few minutes. He seemed to think he ought to see you straight away."

"Thanks for letting me know, Deeley." Mayo broke the connection and then rang down to the front desk, instructing them to send the solicitor up to his office immediately he arrived. If Geoffrey Crytch—of Crytch, Masterson and Crytch, a pleasant, elderly man with whom he'd had one or two dealings—thought it was important, that was enough for Mayo.

"An appalling thing to have happened, appalling," were Crytch's first conventionally expressed words on entering Mayo's room. He had come straight round from his office, which was just along the road from the police station, and though he must have hurried, he was puffing only slightly. A plump man with a deep double chin, well past sixty, silver-haired and well-preserved, he had the milky, replete look of a well-fed baby and a look of mild surprise, maybe at having married a woman much younger than he was, a doctor in professional practice, and having produced, so late in life, a family now just out of their teens. These ingenuous externals were at variance with the sharp mind Mayo knew him to have and a propensity, not usually attributable to solicitors, for getting things done.

They shook hands and Crytch thanked him for seeing him and came straight to the point without waste of time, explaining, in the fruity voice that served him so well in court, that Mrs. Dove had made an appointment to see him at two that afternoon. "When she hadn't turned up by four, my secretary decided she'd better speak to her and find out whether we'd got our dates crossed. Your policeman who answered the phone told her the dreadful news but quite rightly wouldn't give any detail. Are you at liberty to do so?"

"There's no reason why you shouldn't know—I'm sorry to have to tell you Mrs. Dove's been murdered."

"Murdered? Surely not!" Crytch looked shaken to the core, and his complexion abruptly lost some of its rosiness. The presence of the police at the lockhouse must have prepared him and alerted him to the fact that more than a simple death had occurred, however. He sat deep in thought for a while, before suggesting tentatively, "It couldn't have been an accident?"

"It was no accident, she was strangled."

"Good God!"

"You knew her well, I take it?"

"Yes, indeed. Very well. The firm have looked after the Dove family since before I was born. My grandfather first acted for them, if I remember rightly." He hesitated. Presumably, being a solicitor, caution was second nature to him. Presumably he also believed it was good tactics to be completely honest with the police. "Actually, I knew Marion better than that. We were going out together at one time—only a boy and girl romance, but I always hoped when I came back home after the war she'd become my wife. Unfortunately, it didn't quite work out that way."

"Changed her mind, did she?"

Crytch spread plump white hands. "She seemed to lose interest. People change . . . at any rate, she did. In fact, it surprised me she married at all. I'd have laid bets on it she'd have stayed single." He smiled wryly. "Well, she didn't—and in the end she did better for herself by marrying Wesley Dove rather than me."

It sounded as if the memory might have been rather painful, all the same. No man likes to admit rejection, even after forty years. They'd all been young once, these elderly people, Geoffrey Crytch, Marion Dove, Gwen Bainbridge, their blood had run hot. You had to remember that.

Giving Mayo an assessing look, Crytch said carefully, "In view of what you've just told me, I don't think I should be stepping out of line if I told you why she wanted to see me today. She was a woman of some substance, I expect you know that by now . . . well, she'd suddenly taken it into her head she ought to give some of it away to charity and wanted to discuss ways and means with me. I suggested the best way was probably by deed of covenant, and she said, rather curiously I thought, that she was thinking of more immediate arrangements." He paused, thoughtfully. "Strangled? There's no question about that?"

"No question at all. It certainly wasn't suicide, Mr. Crytch."

Mayo was beginning to wonder if he'd found the explanation for the sums Mrs. Dove had recently drawn from her bank account, but on reflection that struck him as fairly unlikely. Surely, she would have made out cheques, not donated such large amounts in cash. "So that was what your appointment today was about?"

"Not entirely. As a matter of fact," Crytch said, "as a matter of fact, she told me she also wanted to make some changes to her will."

At that moment, the tea Mayo had requested came in, brought by a shirt-sleeved constable. After he'd left, Mayo poured two cups and handed one to Crytch, who sipped thirstily at it. The cup rattled slightly as he put it back on the saucer.

"Now that's a very interesting fact, Mr. Crytch. Did she give any indication as to how she was going to change it?"

"No. No, she said she'd explain when she saw me. No great changes, and she'd already worked out a rough draft on paper. . . . You may possibly," he suggested carefully, "have come across it?" It was a question which Mayo chose to evade by regarding it as a statement.

"I wonder who else she told?" he said.

"That's something I'm hardly in a position to know." But would dearly like to know, Mayo thought, and wondered why.

His mind began again to run on those sums the dead woman
had drawn out—and also to play around lightly with notions of
the opportunities solicitors had to fiddle.

"You realize that if this change in her will was to someone's
disadvantage, and he learned about it, that could be a strong
motive for murder?"

"I do realize that," Crytch answered stiffly, "that's why I came
to see you."

"What are the terms of her will as it stands?"

Crytch *ummed* and *aahed* at that. Having gone further than
perhaps he thought cautious, he now began to stand on his professional dignity and said he couldn't possibly breach his client's
confidentiality, but in the end he went so far as to promise that if
the main beneficiaries agreed, he would let Mayo know the
terms of the will as soon as possible, if that would suit him. It
would. If past experience was anything to go by, they would fall
over backwards to demonstrate their willingness to cooperate,
afraid that refusal might throw them under suspicion. But it
wasn't principally *what* was in the will that concerned Mayo—it
was the question of who might have been disadvantaged by any
alterations, and the answer to that, apparently, had been only in
the mind of the dead woman.

Not long after Crytch had left, Kite came on the line.

"I've been hanging about here waiting for Paul Fish to come
home from school. Then his dad arrives and says he's gone,
scarpered. He went off this Monday morning, told him he
doesn't know when he'll be back."

"Where are you? Still at Stubbs Road? Stay where you are,"
Mayo told him, "I'll join you as soon as I can."

Stubbs Road clung tenaciously to the side of a hill, a road in a
pre-war housing estate which the council, against much opposition, had sold off at favourable prices to sitting tenants. Most of
the houses, small and semi-detached, with a forest of TV aerials
sprouting from the chimneys, had had a miscellany of improve-
ments added by way of garages or car-ports, bay windows and
porches. Bull's-eye glass, and stone facings put on to what had
been grey pebble-dash were much in evidence, and most were
smartly painted.

Number 47 had once upon a time had its pebble-dash snow-

cemmed in beige and its paintwork done blue, but by now most
of that was a memory. Dandelion and twitch were breaking up
the short concrete front path and the front gate was hardly visible under a tangle of quickthorn, indicating its long disuse, so
Mayo pushed open the side gate that warned *Beware of the Dog.*
The warning was superfluous. As soon as his hand had touched
the latch a Staffordshire bull terrier, the ugliest he'd ever seen
outside the pages of the *Beano,* a caricature of rage and ferocity,
began to raise hell from a barred kennel strong enough to cage a
tiger, with "Caesar" painted crudely in white over its opening.

Mayo trusted the neighbours were deaf. He knocked loudly
enough to hope he'd be heard above the din, with the dog
choking on the chain behind him. It was Kite who opened the
door. As he stepped inside, a powerful combination of old fry-
ing fat and stale cigarette smoke solid enough to cut with a knife
almost made him reel. Charlie Fish was sitting at the kitchen
table with his head in his hands, in a welter of dirty coffee mugs
and cold greasy plates bearing the remains of old junk-food
meals, the one on the table containing some congealed chips and
the remains of a piece of battered fish. A pile of used crockery
was jumbled into the sink, along with old teabags and a grey
dishcloth of uncertain provenance. On the drainer was about
two pounds of good quality beef, some of it already cut up and
put into the dog's dish. What kind of man would buy rump steak
for his dog and live off fish and chips himself?

Kite leaned against the wall. "Isn't there anywhere else we
can talk?" Mayo asked, revolted.

"What for?" Fish raised a bleary unshaven face and breathed
out beer fumes strong enough to deduce that his posture was
more likely to be due to a thick head than despair. He blinked,
his eyes focused on Mayo's cold grey gaze, and he shrugged.
"Oh, orright. Come on into the lounge."

"I'd get some black coffee down you first to pull yourself
together, if I were you."

"I don't need no coffee." Fish shambled gracelessly out of the
kitchen, through the passageway and into the room he euphe-
mistically called the lounge. It was only slightly less squalid than
the kitchen. Flinging himself on to a sofa transmogrified to mud-
colour and scarred on the arms with old cigarette burns, he lit

up again, while the two policemen gingerly found places on the
least encumbered of the grease-spotted armchairs.

"Well, what you wanting?"

Mayo regarded the unprepossessing specimen of humanity
before him without charity. Charlie Fish, properly dressed and
reasonably sober, could still have been handsome in a dark,
gypsy sort of way. He had a head of curly black hair, at present
overlong and unkempt, and a raffish, foxy look that might once
have been attractive to a certain type of woman, but the years
had coarsened his features, a beer belly rolled over the belt that
held his trousers up.

"Where's your wife?" Mayo asked.

"My wife? Norma?" Fish laughed unpleasantly. "How the
hell should I know? Buggered off with the TV man seven or
eight years ago her did, and nobody's seen hide nor hair of her
since. Story of my life, that is. They all leave me. First her. Then
my eldest lad, every encouragement to get to bloody university,
then too bloody stuck up to come back home once he's there.
Now Paul."

"I'm crying my eyes out," Kite said. "What's your other son's
name? Steven?"

"No, it's not. It's Graham. Why?"

"Never mind. Is Paul in touch with his mother?" Mayo asked.

"You must be joking! Her left him when he was eight years
old—wouldn't know one another from Adam now. Anyway,
what's it to you? What is all this?"

"You've no idea at all where he could have gone?"

"He don't tell me nothink—I'm only his father."

"Didn't you ask him why he was going—or try and stop
him?"

Fish shrugged. "He's old enough to please hisself. He's seventeen."

Mayo held on to his disgust and asked shortly whether it was
likely that Paul could be with his brother, but clearly Charlie
Fish had no notion. He evidently had little idea how his son had
spent his time, nor, it seemed, did he care. They were nominally
father and son, they occupied the same house but might have
existed on different planets. Poor little devil, Mayo thought.
What sort of chances could they ever have, kids like this, what
values were they expected to learn? He gave up the idea of

questioning Fish as a bad job and asked if they could see Paul's
room.

"Not unless you tell me what all this is about. You can't come
in here, just like that, without no search warrant, I know me
rights."

"Cut it out, Fish. We're on a murder enquiry."

"What's that got to do with our Paul? Here, hold *on*—"

"Last night, Marion Dove was murdered. That's your wife's
aunt, in case you'd forgotten."

"Forgotten that bloody lot? Not likely! It's her and them
Bainbridges between 'em as have put all these fancy ideas into
my lads' heads. Interfering old buggers."

"You just watch your language, or we might just decide to
have *you* in for insulting behaviour—or even on suspicion." The
craven fear that sprang into Fish's face as Mayo said this made
him pause. "You didn't do it, did you, Fish?" he asked softly.
"You knew she was well off, you didn't go there on Sunday
morning demanding money and then kill her when she refused?"

"No! No, I never did! I was up the Dog, Sunday morning!"

"The Dog and Fox, eh? Not a million miles from the Jubilee!
In fact, less than half a mile on the Compsall Road."

"I was in the pub, I tell you, till they closed. Anybody'll tell
you."

"And after they closed?"

"I was here, having a kip, wasn't I? Then back to the Dog,
Sunday night."

"And after *that?*"

"It's got sod all to do with you, but I was with—somebody
else."

"Oh yes, who?" Fish said nothing. "Who?" repeated Mayo.
"Who were you with?"

"Right, then, I was with Ruby Deacon. Orright?"

"Ruby Deacon! Dear oh dear!" What sort of alibi was that?
She'd say anything for tuppence, that one, do anything, some
said. A hard case. "Come off it, Fish, don't make me laugh.
You'll have to do better than that. And while you have another
think, we'll go and have a look at Paul's room."

They'd hit on something, Mayo felt sure, though whether it
had anything to do with Marion Dove's murder he was less sure.

At any rate, Fish became suddenly, if not more cooperative, at least less obstructive. Reduced to silence, he stood sullenly aside and let them pass up the narrow staircase. By chance the first door they opened turned out to be Paul's bedroom. Sparsely furnished, a single bed covered by a red blanket tidily tucked in, and a small dressing table that evidently served as a desk, with a chair in front and on it a pile of exercise books with "Paul Fish" printed on the cover. Its neatness, in contrast with the rooms downstairs, made it seem almost monastic, but any bareness was dissipated by the squadrons of model aircraft dancing from the ceiling on cotton threads, and the photographs and drawings, all of them representing aircraft of some description, which nearly covered the shabby old Snoopy wallpaper. A home-made bookshelf held a row of library books and paperbacks. Mayo recalled with what passionate intensity as a schoolboy he'd pursued the hobby of the moment, to the exclusion of everything else: model railways, stamp collecting, all the usual things. Though by seventeen, he reckoned, he'd outgrown most of them. He reached up and touched one of the models. It was clean enough, with only a light film of dust, and so were the others. Some of the library books had current date stamps. *Aircraft of the World; Learning to Fly; Enemy Coast Ahead.* Farnborough, Sheila Scott, Neville Duke.

Kite said, opening the cupboard in one corner, "If he's gone for good, he hasn't taken all his clothes." Sportsgear piled up in one corner and a school blazer hanging up beside a pair of dark grey school trousers were understandably left behind, but there were also jeans and T-shirts, underclothes, a pair of nearly new shoes and some trainers.

Mayo replaced *Flight Briefing for Pilots* and looked out of the window. The streets of the estate were in tiers; the downstairs windows of the street above looked directly into the bedroom windows of the one below. Between were tiny gardens crammed with sheds and greenhouses, rabbit hutches, swings and dustbins. The only space and freedom was in the empty skies above. He said, "I'm going over to see Mrs. Bainbridge. You can come with me. She saw Paul on Sunday night, when he took her home, didn't she? And I shall want Forensics up here to take some of Paul's prints."

The same unspoken thought, of the five hundred pounds, as

yet unaccounted for, passed between them. Kite said, "What you just said to Fish, downstairs, it went home. Think he knows something?"

"I wouldn't bank on it—but he's up to something diabolical, you can bet your boot soles. One of our customers, is he?"

"Not to my knowledge."

"Well, whichever way up, he's a nasty piece of work. So watch him. Don't let him slip."

"No way," grinned Kite, "it'll be a pleasure."

Yes, they kept the car in one of the lock-up garages round the corner. Paul had keys, both for the garage and the car—but he always came and asked permission before he took it out, always. As Mrs. Bainbridge gave Kite her key, her hand trembled.

But of course, the fifteen-year-old Mini had gone.

"Now think back to when you saw him Sunday night, Mrs. Bainbridge," Mayo said. "That was just after half past ten, right?" She nodded miserably. "How did he seem—different, or just as usual?"

"He was in a state," she admitted at last. "I could tell there was something the matter. He hadn't long passed his test, but he usually drove very careful, at least when I was with him, but Sunday night he was, you know, erratic, grinding the gears and jamming the brakes on. I told him to go steady and he did, I don't think he realized how badly he'd been driving."

"And?"

"That's all. I asked him what was wrong, but he said there was nothing the matter. I didn't push it, I thought it was likely another row with that Charlie Fish and least said about it the better."

"You were right about that anyway, they had had an argument, his father admits it." Fish had insisted it was nothing more than the usual row. Paul had asked for some spending money, his father had refused. It was the same old set-to they had every week. He'd get over it, he always did. Did Paul think he was made of lousy money? He was unemployed and had been living on social security for years. Anyhow, he knew for a fact that Marion Dove was in the habit of slipping Paul the odd fiver or so for the jobs he did for her, so why should he subsidise him as well?

"Was the tank full?" Kite asked. "He might not have had much money, in which case he can't have got far . . . what's the matter, Mrs. Bainbridge?"

Her hand had gone to her mouth. "It's just—I've remembered—my Visa card's missing. I thought I'd lost it—the clasp on my bag's not very clever—and I was going to report it, but with all that's happened today that was the last thing I was thinking about . . . oh, my God."

"Could Paul have taken it?"

"He'd never do a thing like that!"

"Did he have the opportunity?"

After a moment she reluctantly admitted it was possible. "He came in with me for a coffee when we got home. I went straight upstairs to see that Robert was all right, but he was still asleep. I left my bag on the kitchen table while I went upstairs . . ."

Mayo said, "We'll have a stop put on your card, and if Paul does try to use it, that'll help us to find him."

In a moment of unprofessional but spontaneous sympathy, Kite put his arm round her shoulder as they were leaving. "Don't worry, m'duck, he might have run away for all sorts of reasons." It wasn't what he thought himself, but he didn't see any point in increasing her alarm and anxiety.

Chapter nine

The cheese rolls from the canteen were more than usually uninspired, and the coffee was anaemic. A pile of work, not all of it connected with the present case, was waiting on Mayo's desk. The air conditioning seemed to be going berserk. His office was like an oven.

"What are they trying to do, suffocate us?" Mayo flung open the window and the door, and slung his jacket over the back of a chair. It was only seven o'clock and it was already beginning to feel like the end of a very long day.

On the same principle as he'd used as a child, when eating his greens or liver first and saving the chips until last, he put the day's reports on one side and looked through the other documents, unmistakably the work of Atkins, without doubt the most economical user of typewriter ribbons and punctuation in the whole of the Lavenstock police force. Deciphering them as he masticated his way through the cheese rolls, he saw that two of them concerned missing young people. One girl disappearing—nasty, that always gave him a sinking feeling—and one boy turning up. Another latter-day Dick Whittington, this one, looking not for fame and fortune, but freedom and excitement in the big city. One of the thousands, heartbreak left in his wake, and appeals on the London Underground to ring home with no strings attached. Was this in fact all that had happened to Paul Fish? Well, this particular Whittington had had enough of sleeping rough, running out of money, not enough to eat. He'd turned and come home, disillusioned. Maybe Paul would, too.

They'd barely finished eating when Cherry rang down and spoke to Mayo. Before he went home to his supper, the superintendent wanted updating on the present case, and also a word about his own attendance, together with Mayo in court the next morning, where they were required to give evidence in a case

concerning a series of organised shoplifting from local super-
markets. He wanted to get home himself, he said, so he'd not
take up more than ten minutes of Mayo's time. Which meant
half an hour, Mayo reckoned, if Cherry was hungry, three quar-
ters if not.

"Home!" Mayo grunted as he put the receiver back, annoyed
at being reminded of the time he was going to have to waste in
court tomorrow, something he'd been trying hard not to remember all day. "We'll be lucky if we get there before midnight."

For a while after he'd left the office, Kite sat mulling over
what they'd discussed. Then he picked up the telephone and
dialled. He announced himself to the woman at the other end
and after her surprised reaction asked, "Fiona, is Colin there?"

He was told that he was not.

"What, still down at school at this time? Them's policeman's
hours!" he joked.

"I know," Fiona Massey answered rather crisply.

Kite knew all about that tone of voice. Not that he heard it
too often nowadays, now that Sheila had her own career to occupy her and little time to dwell on the injustices of being a
policeman's wife, but when he did, he knew it was time to wave
the white flag.

Fiona went on to explain that some new schedules or other
that Colin worked on during the holidays weren't going according to plan and needed adjustments. He'd tried bringing the
work home, but what with three kids under his feet, he'd packed
in the idea and decided staying on at school was a better bet
after all. It was all right for some, wasn't it?

"Well, thanks, I'll go down and see him there," Kite rejoined
hastily. "Promise I won't keep him too long! Take care, love.
Bye."

"If the gaffer wants me," he said to the sergeant on the front
desk as he went out, "tell him I'll be back within the hour."

Colin Massey was sandy-haired and bearded, a big rawboned
man of Scottish descent whose appearance brought Porage Oat
packets and the skirl of the bagpipes irresistibly to mind. He and
Kite had been at school together. The friendship had continued
after they left, and been strong enough to survive the separation

of Colin's university years but had, like so many other things since Kite had joined the police force, and even more since he joined the CID, lapsed somewhat. He was now deputy headmaster at the Comprehensive, and although the times they now saw each other were fairly infrequent, the two men never found any difficulty in picking up where they had left off. He was delighted to see Kite again and said he was quite prepared to help, sure he was, nevertheless his response became guarded when he learned who it was Kite was enquiring about.

"Paul Fish? A quiet lad, a bit of a dreamer. Likeable enough though." He leaned back in his chair at full stretch, his hands in the pockets of his corduroys and heels dug into the hairy tiles that carpeted his room. "Well, you could say *very* likeable, considering his background."

"I've seen something of that."

"Then you'll know what I mean. Why do you want to know? Not in trouble, is he, Martin?"

"I hope not. Didn't you know he hasn't been at school these last two days?"

"No, but I wouldn't. He's only with me on Thursdays this term."

"It looks very much as though he may have done a bunk."

"Oh. Oh Lord, has he?"

Kite looked at him sharply. "You don't sound surprised."

"Should I be? With a father like that?"

Kite soon found out that Massey was familiar not only with Paul's immediate family circumstances but also knew of his connection with Mrs. Dove and the Bainbridges. He watched his friend's face lengthen as he told him what he knew of the situation. "So tell me anything you can about Paul, will you, Colin? Anything you think might help."

"Well . . ." The schoolmaster tugged at his beard and thought. "Scholastically he's only average, in fact he came a cropper in his O levels. He re-sat a couple and did better, and now he's determined to get good A grades. He won't manage it, I'm bound to say, never mind beat Graham . . . that's his brother. Very bright indeed, Graham, but a hard act to follow. He could've made it to Oxbridge, but he couldn't be dissuaded from Northumbria—not entirely uninfluenced by the fact that his girlfriend was going there, I imagine, but mainly because they've a particularly good fine arts course up there."

That was where Rachel Dove lectured, Kite recalled. University of Northumbria, situated midway between York and Durham. "Are they close, the brothers? I'm wondering if Paul might have gone up there."

"The university term doesn't start until mid-October, remember, and anyway, I happen to know Graham's in China."

"China?"

"It's the latest student thing. Getting there's the main problem, but once there, food and transport costs are dirt cheap by our standards, they sleep travelling on the trains . . . yes, I suppose the two boys are close in a way. Paul's crazy about flying, did you know?" he added, with seeming inconsequence. Kite said he'd guessed. "I've sometimes wondered if that's what it's all about—sibling rivalry and all that sort of thing—if he can't beat Graham one way, he'll do it another. He hasn't really a hope of getting a university place anywhere, if we're being honest. Actually, I think he's admitted it to himself deep down."

The room faced over the playing fields and a netball court where a group of fourteen or fifteen year old girls were playing an energetic and noisy after-school game. Girls of all shapes and sizes, some slender and graceful, some hearty and heavy footed, still burdened with puppy fat. Echoes of their shouts floated through the open window, the sun, low in the sky, flashed on heated faces and young limbs.

"This flying's a bit more than a hobby with him, isn't it?" Kite asked.

"It's an obsession. I didn't know about it until I had him in for a heart-to-heart when he flunked his 0 levels. I got him talking about himself, the usual thing, what he wanted to do with his life, what his interests were and so on. I'd never got near him before, but suddenly, wham, there it was—the only thing he cared a jot about. Flying. Apparently this Bainbridge uncle was a rear-gunner in the war and it seems they talk about nothing else. He's encouraged Paul to the extent where he's even fantasising about having flying lessons. I told him not to get his feet off the ground, if you'll pardon the pun, reminded him the lessons cost a fortune, but he said no, Mrs. Dove had promised to pay for them when he was eighteen."

"She had?"

"That's what he said . . . the only snag was there were conditions attached, and they went very much against the grain."

"What conditions?"

"She wanted him to join the family firm when he left school. Definitely not what Paul has in mind. He's got one idea in his head when it comes to thinking of a career—and that's not concerned with making glass. I could see it wasn't a lot of use reminding him that in the present climate plenty of kids would give their eye teeth to have a job like that waiting for them when they left school, not to mention one with such prospects—which I imagine would mean he'd eventually have enough cash to fly all he wanted—but when I pointed this out, it cut no ice, I doubt he was even listening."

Perhaps, thought Kite, he was thinking of that promised legacy of his great-aunt's. If Shirley Dainty had told the truth about it perhaps that, and the flying lessons—without conditions attached, had suddenly seemed accessible. Or what if she'd told him she'd decided *not* to leave him anything in her new will if he wouldn't promise to go into the firm? Fed up with his father, that might have been the last straw. He asked abruptly, "Would you say he could be a violent lad?"

Massey replied with careful qualification, "Not under normal circumstances, but you can never really tell with adolescents. They can become emotionally disturbed over what might appear to be trifles. It's a hell of a time for them, particularly with today's pressures. They're not kids any longer, but they're expected to be adults before they've the maturity to cope with it."

"Yes." Kite watched a young Amazon raising the ball high in front of her to shoot into the net. When he was fifteen he'd been desperately in love with a girl like that, a blonde with long legs and big, bouncing breasts. "Remember Maxine Thompson, Colin?"

Massey followed his glance and grinned. "She's a physiotherapist up at the hospital now."

"Wouldn't you know."

He'd privately thought himself no end of a lad at that age. But in public, that was different. Desperately unsure of himself, abashed at the size of his hands and feet, his clumsiness and his sprouting moustache . . . it hadn't helped when the lovely

Maxine had rejected him for a wimp named Julian Something-or-other, a pimply undersized youth with greasy locks, and he could remember even now the burning humiliation, the painful sense of rejection, the strong desire to grind Julian Something-or-other between his back teeth and spit him out in little bits. Adolescence was one hell of a time.

Kite drove back to Milford Road and told Mayo what had transpired. "He's evidently been under a lot of pressure lately, from one direction or another. It's conceivable he may have found it all too much."

"All right, Mrs. Dove was putting pressure on him to join the firm, but it wasn't imminent, he still has another year at school. And we've no evidence at all that he was anywhere near the lockhouse that weekend. We can't go around suspecting him until we have."

It also seemed to Mayo that it was a point in Paul's favour that if Mrs. Dove had been dead by the time her sister rang her at one-thirty, and Paul *had* been responsible and had subsequently made off with the missing five hundred pounds, then he would hardly have pestered his father afterwards for the few pounds he may or may not have got from him.

Kite said, "I've got a list of some of his friends from Colin Massey. I'll get somebody on to it tomorrow, see if we can get a lead on what he was doing."

He could leave it to Kite. For himself, Mayo couldn't summon up much interest for pursuing something he didn't really want to pursue. Not because Paul's youth made the possibility unlikely—doubts about that kind of objection had taken a nose dive long ago in the teeth of evidence to the contrary—and he'd do it if he had do, but he'd need to be more convinced than he was at present.

All the same, there *were* disturbing lines of connection between Paul and Marion Dove.

It was indeed after midnight when they finally called it a day.

Kite drove home to his semi-detached house on a private estate at the edge of the town, left the car in the drive and let himself into the bright kitchen he'd recently redecorated. As a finishing touch, Sheila had persuaded him to invest in a micro-

wave oven, a boon, she'd argued, for getting the children a
quick meal when she came in late, and with Kite working the
odd hours he did. So far he'd steered clear of it, but the effect of
the cheese rolls had long since worn off and he was starving, and
Sheila had left a note to say there was a chicken casserole in the
fridge which just needed heating up if he fancied it. It really did
heat up in the incredibly short space of time the instructions said
it would, and with no kids around to set a bad example to he
polished it off straight from the dish.

On his way upstairs he looked into his sons' room, as he always did. Daniel, on the top bunk, was flat on his stomach as
usual and Davy, also as usual, was invisible in a mighty tangle of
bedclothes. How could a duvet get tied into a knot? He didn't
attempt to untangle his son; in a few minutes he'd be in the same
state again.

"What time is it?" Sheila murmured sleepily as he crept into
bed, her curly brown head just visible above the sheets. "Ouch,
your feet are freezing, you've been walking about without shoes
again."

"I didn't want to disturb you."

"Why not?" she asked. Warming his feet with her own, she
turned towards him and lifted her face and curled her small
warm body into his arms.

Mayo couldn't sleep. He had, over the years, taught himself
to relax at will, snatching sleep and rest when he could, but
tonight his technique wasn't working. He'd done himself some
half-hearted beans on toast and then been too tired to taste them
and now he lay unsleeping, the events of the case turning over
and over in his mind no matter how he tried to blank them out.
He tried thinking of other things, but that was worse. The
cheerful optimism with which he'd returned from holiday now
seemed quite unjustified. He'd only had the chance of a few
unsatisfactory words with Alex during the day, but looking back
on them, he couldn't recall that she had appeared to have missed
him unduly while he'd been away.

Damn these self-sufficient, career-minded women. And yet,
wasn't that what he wanted? Lynne had been content to be a
housewife and mother, without outside interests of her own,
dependent on him for companionship and resentful of a job that

wasn't nine to five, and the tensions had become unbearable. Poor Lynne. If she hadn't died, the marriage would inevitably sooner or later have ended in divorce, he knew it. Paradoxically, that would perhaps have left him less guilt-ridden. As it was, her pert little face that had turned sharp and discontented with the years, the soft voice that had too often become a whingeing monotone haunted him yet.

He finally gave up the attempt to sleep altogether, turned on the light and picked up his current book. In a few minutes, he was fast asleep.

Chapter ten

"The PM report's in, sir," Kite announced, looking up from his first half-pint of coffee of the morning. "It's on your desk."

Timpson-Ludgate had come up with no surprises. The substance of the report was that Marion Elizabeth Dove, sixty-two years of age and suffering from advanced carcinoma of the liver, had died by manual strangulation, prior to the body being immersed in the canal for some thirty-six to forty-eight hours before it had been taken out on Tuesday morning. Examination of the stomach contents showed that a small quantity of toast and some tea had been consumed a few hours before death. Reasonable then to work on the assumption it had been breakfast, and that death had occurred on Sunday morning, some time between then and one-thirty, when her sister had rung. No traces of skin or fibre had been found under her nails to indicate she had fought her attacker . . . no bruises were reported, other than where heavy hands had gripped her upper arms, before moving on to her throat. There was considerable bruising there, and enough force had been used to break the hyoid bone; her age, however, made it probable that this, situated just above the Adam's apple, was brittle and therefore easily broken.

There'd been no indication of any great struggle on the canal bank, either, Mayo recalled. It was almost as though she hadn't *tried* to defend herself.

Later, Mayo dutifully presented himself at court along with Cherry, prepared for a long and tedious morning. He wasn't in for any surprises there, either, and it wasn't until after lunch that he was free to make his way to the glassworks. He'd learned that Ken Dainty would be closeted with important customers that afternoon and was not to be disturbed unless it was absolutely necessary. So it was business as usual, was it, the small matter of his wife's mother being killed wasn't going to change anything. To be fair though, Dainty wasn't going to achieve anything by letting his affairs go to pot—and his wife would have her sister with her now. While Mayo wouldn't have had any compunction in bringing Dainty from his meeting had it suited him, he'd decided to leave him for the time being and instead made arrangements to see Mr. Bainbridge. He suspected that in any case at this point he'd probably get more of what he wanted from him than Dainty.

The factory, just off the main road, with a glimpse of water, the now disused arm of the canal, running behind it, could best have been described as a fine example of Victorian sham. Behind the elegant and impressive wrought iron gates with their intertwined doves, a shabby, haphazard collection of old buildings was roughly grouped together, in dire need of smartening up. The office block was about on a par, the reception area reminiscent of dentists' waiting rooms, with a glassed-in switchboard cubicle in the corner and a concession to the nature of their business in the form of a showcase where various pieces of crystal were displayed against dark blue velvet.

Business, however, was brisk. He had to wait several minutes before the telephonist was free, a girl with the face of a Botticelli angel, blonde curls, and a skin like painted porcelain, chiming "Dove's-Glass-can-I-*help*-yew?" as if she were wound up by a little key in her back. At last another girl appeared to lead him to Mr. Bainbridge. She was plump and rather plain, but the intelligence in her face, and her silence, were a change after the Botticelli angel. Twice as they progressed upstairs he thought she was going to speak, but she was young and he guessed she found the situation embarrassing and didn't quite know what to say to him in the circumstances. She showed him into an office next door to where he'd been received yesterday and had imparted the news of Mrs. Dove's death. Not anywhere near as spacious, but light and pleasant, with a high ceiling and the desk placed so that Bainbridge had the same, though narrower, view that Ken had.

Mayo suspected this was not a good day for the old man. He had almost asked him not to bother getting up as he was shown into the room, but saw in time that his consideration would not have been appreciated. Robert Bainbridge evidently chose not to spare himself. An authoritative figure behind his desk or when moving by the aid of strategically placed pieces of furniture, his lameness was not as apparent as it had been when he had met them yesterday in the outer office, leaning on his stick. What it cost him to keep up his self-imposed discipline was anybody's guess—to reach this office, there were two flights of steep stairs and no lifts. Negotiating them must be a twice-daily feat of heroism, but work, a view of himself as a still-useful member of society, being a lynchpin here in the office, Mayo could see, that would be more important to a man like Bainbridge. It was something he understood. He worked better under tension himself, it kept the adrenaline going and pushed you further than you knew you could go.

"Is there any news of the boy?" were Bainbridge's first words.

Mayo told him they were doing their best, but nothing had transpired so far. "But I'd like to take this opportunity of having a few words with you about him. As I understand it, you probably know him better than anyone else." He studied the man's face as he spoke, with its deeply moulded contours, spare and bleached as a bone, its deep-set eyes regarding him shrewdly. The face was severe with pain but Mayo saw evidence of an ironic humour and perhaps a wry kindliness there.

"Do I? Yes. Yes, I suppose I do. We talk—or rather he lets me talk, about my flying days, you know. There are few people who are interested in one's wartime exploits, but Paul's an appreciative audience. I can understand that—aeroplanes have always had a fascination for me, too." He had a precise, pedantic way of speaking, either natural or more likely something he'd acquired as part of his persona as office patriarch.

"You didn't feel that you were perhaps over-encouraging him?"

"I don't think that's possible. 'A man's reach should exceed his grasp—or what's Heaven for?' Isn't that what the poet said?"

Mayo wasn't sure that the analogy would stand up. It was one thing to encourage the young to aim high, but not so high that, like the young Icarus, they burned their wings on the sun. He said, "Why do you think he's disappeared?"

"Not because he's killed Marion. That's not possible," Bainbridge said flatly. "He was extremely fond of her, and anyway, he's not that sort of boy. His home life isn't very satisfactory, as you're no doubt aware, but he doesn't make that an excuse to act the young tearaway. He's a decent boy and I gather he's had another row with his father, which always upsets him. He'll come back when he's got it out of his system."

He spoke with such calm assurance, his intense dark eyes, deeply contrasting with his pale polished face, looking over the half-moon glasses, intelligent and alert, that it was difficult not to be carried along by his positiveness.

Mayo said, "He's disappeared though, hasn't be? Apparently with your car and your wife's Visa card. We also have reason to believe there's a large amount of money missing from Mrs. Dove's possession."

Bainbridge regarded him steadily. "I stand by what I said. Paul could never have murdered Marion."

At that point, the tea Mr. Bainbridge had asked for was brought in by the girl who'd shown him up. "Thank you, Valerie, perhaps you wouldn't mind . . ."

Conversation lapsed during the business of pouring the tea, settling whether milk and sugar was required. When the girl had gone, casting him another of those slightly agonised looks, Mayo began again by asking Bainbridge how long he'd worked at Dove's.

The answer came promptly. "Forty-four years to be exact." Stirring sugar into his tea he leaned back, seeming glad that Mayo was not pursuing the question of Paul and the missing money. "I'd always intended to go in for accountancy but the war put a stop to that. It needn't have done, there was no lack of schemes for training ex-servicemen, but I'd spent the last eighteen months of the war getting myself patched up and there wasn't much energy left for raising new initiatives. When Wesley Dove offered me a job in his office, I thought why not?" He smiled faintly. "I took it as a stop gap, later I turned it to my advantage and learned to enjoy it for its own sake."

Yes, he'd know all about the company, everything that went on, which Mayo had counted on. But . . . he might not tell. He looked like a man who could keep secrets.

"Funny how things happen," Bainbridge mused, encouraged to continue by the apparently unhurried attitude Mayo was prepared to assume to hide his contained impatience. "I never intended coming back to Lavenstock after the war. At nineteen, it seemed a dump to me and I couldn't wait to shake the dust off my feet. Then when I saw it the morning after that bad raid, that was it. I suddenly realized how much the place meant to me—it was my town and I knew I'd come back despite everything and settle down. Gwennie and I were going to be married and I decided then and there we weren't going to wait. We were only nineteen. Too young? In wartime it didn't seem so. Nor has it ever." A smile, fleeting and brilliant as a shooting star, lit his eyes. "I've been a very fortunate man, Mr. Mayo."

Mayo was reminded of his wife's face when she had spoken of him. They'd been married—how long?—forty-odd years? And still considered themselves lucky. Unaccountably, Mayo felt left out in the cold.

"You didn't meet your wife in the forces then?"

"We'd known each other by sight all our lives but it wasn't until we found ourselves on the same RAF station that we got to know each other—and fell in love. Things being what they were of course we were immediately posted to different parts of the country! Our leaves never seemed to coincide—but that's the fortunes of war. Good fortune sometimes—she'd just been posted and her leave cancelled, otherwise she'd have been home too when the bomb fell."

"I hadn't realized there was enemy action in Lavenstock."

"Not if you're comparing it with Coventry, but enough for a small town. It wasn't good that night. The house in Chapel Street was hit, her parents taken to hospital with minor injuries. When Gwennie heard, she applied for compassionate leave but she was stationed in the north of Scotland and didn't get home straight away, so young Marion had to cope alone. You could tell she was very shocked, but she was exceedingly brave. But then, she always was. She had her own inner resources, even then. She never deserved what she got."

A small silence fell. The tea was drunk, it seemed appropriate to begin more immediate questions. He felt Bainbridge was a shrewd observer and would be an impartial witness. "Do you have any suspicions at all as to who might have killed her?" he asked. When asked that particular question direct, it was surprising how many people responded with answers which often led to the truth.

Bainbridge picked up his pen and rolled it between his steepled fingers, considering. "I've thought it over, naturally, but I've come to the conclusion that it would be invidious to suppose anyone close would be capable of such malice towards her."

"What about others? Had there been trouble with anyone here, for instance?"

"Not to my knowledge—and I'm sure I would have known if there was."

"Well then, let's talk about Mrs. Dove herself, if you don't mind, sir."

"Not at all. I'll say straight away it's been a great shock, not only to my wife and myself, but to everyone here, too. Dove's is above all a family concern and we were all of us deeply fond of Marion."

"I believe she took an active part in the business until recently?"

Bainbridge inclined his head and said she had, until two years ago. When she reached sixty, she had thought it time to retire, though for some time before that, she'd been leaving things more and more to Mr. Dainty. "Quite rightly. He's very capable, very sound."

"She'd some idea of young Paul coming into the company when he left school, I believe?"

"So you've heard about that?" Bainbridge smiled, rather coolly, but didn't ask how Mayo knew. "Well, yes, that was so—but I'm not sure she was right, in this instance. Paul isn't very interested and you really can't impose conditions of that sort. It was understandable, though, she was very concerned, as we all are, with family continuity in the firm. The name of Dove in one form or another has been connected with glassmaking for at least five centuries, did you know that?"

"That's a long time. And now?"

"The name may not be the same, but the tradition will still be there, Mr. Mayo. I know of no other industry with such a proud and continuous history as glassmaking. Nor one so family-orientated, come to that. I suppose it's unique. It's always been the custom for members of one family to work together in teams—'chairs' as they're called. At one time here at Dove's, we'd no less than twenty members of the same family working for us in one capacity or another! Mr. Dainty was part of that particular clan, his father, uncles, grandfather were all blowers here. And in fact, a long way back, they were connected with the Doves through marriage. His two sons are very young yet, but I know he's extremely keen that they'll carry on the tradition."

"Perhaps they'll be like Paul, and won't want to."

"Then he'll be bitterly disappointed. Glassmaking's his whole life, and there's nothing he doesn't know about the business. The firm had unfortunately rather dwindled during Mr. Wesley Dove's last years, but Ken's getting it back on its feet. There's much to be done, but he understands that change for its own sake isn't necessarily a good thing, it's better to make haste slowly, to consolidate and build on what you have. He's doing a splendid job. It would be a great pity if anything were allowed to spoil what he's worked for, but of course that won't happen now that he'll be totally in control."

Mayo caught some nuance of something there, but the significance escaped him. Eventually he said, "How can you be certain he will be?"

"It's never been any secret in the family," Bainbridge answered calmly, "that he was the heir apparent. Old Mr. Wesley, now—he thought he was immortal and would live forever, but in the end he died suddenly and without warning, without making any real provision for who was to follow him. Marion had no intention of allowing that to happen again."

Mayo wondered if Bainbridge realised how he was implicating Dainty by what he'd revealed. He said, his eyes resting on the other man's face, assessingly, "Would it surprise you to know that she intended changing her will?"

"Did she? No, it wouldn't surprise me. I believe the will was made out a long time ago, and as one gets older, circumstances change, time no longer seems infinite. I've felt myself from the age of sixty that every day is a bonus."

"I take it you didn't know Mrs. Dove was seriously ill?"

The other man looked suddenly a little greyer, a little more stooped. "Not until my wife told me. That makes it even more understandable, that she should want to put her affairs in order."

A reminder of mortality briefly silenced both men. "You

don't think the new will might have concerned Mr. Dainty's succession? Could they have disagreed in some way about it?''

"I think it highly unlikely." A faint smile lifted the corners of his mouth. "Firstly because I don't believe, even if she'd told him about any changes she was going to make, that they'd have been substantial enough to affect him. Secondly, because neither has ever been the quarrelling type. Ken would simply bide his time, then try another tack, and Marion could be stubborn on occasions but she'd usually give in rather than have any trouble, which she couldn't bear. She'd had a few words with Gwennie for instance last Friday and it had upset her terribly.''

"Your wife mentioned there'd been an argument."

"Oh, I'd hardly call it an argument, just a difference of opinion. Marion admitted to me she'd been rather tactless. It was nothing, just a few words over a bungalow we'd put in an offer for. I'd had a rather more substantial win than usual last week—I like a harmless little flutter occasionally—and we thought we could manage it, but the price turned out to be way above our heads. Gwennie was rather down in the mouth about it when Marion popped in to see her at the shop, and offered to make up the difference, but I'm afraid Gwennie's always been inclined to be touchy about what she sees as charity and took exception to that.''

So this was where the money went in the Bainbridge household—the "occasional little flutters" which weren't perhaps quite so harmless when they meant his wife going out at nights pulling pints for the locals, at a time of life when she might have expected to stay at home with her knitting. Or when it meant they couldn't afford the bungalow that could mean so much in terms of ease and comfort for them both. He was sure neither of them looked at it in this light, and on the whole this surprising streak of rashness in the pedantic Mr. Bainbridge seemed endearing rather than otherwise, a peccadillo bringing him down to the level of other mortals.

He stood up. "I won't keep you any longer, Mr. Bainbridge. Thank you for being so helpful.''

The girl called Valerie was hanging about in the corridor when he came out. "I'll show you out.''

He smiled at her. "Don't bother. I can find my own way.''

"Oh, it's no bother.''

An uneasy silence hung between them as he followed her down the narrow stairs again. At the foot, she stood hesitating with her hand on the knob of the door into the reception area.

"Was there something you wanted to say to me?"

She gave a sort of gasp and went very pink. "Oh no, only that we're all terribly upset," she said in a rush, tears springing to her eyes, "about Mrs. Dove."

A man in a brown smock came through the door from the other side. "Orright, Val?" he asked, looking curiously at her.

"Yes, thanks, Jim. I-I'm sorry, I have to go now," she said breathlessly to Mayo and turning followed the man quickly up the stairs.

It was after four when he came out into the yard and made his way across to his car. Inserting his key into the lock, he chanced to look up, his eye caught by a flight of pigeons swooping round the tall red-brick house in the garden beyond the wall, the house that was called The Mount.

It was a house that had always interested him as he passed in his car, and since Shirley Dainty had mentioned it, he had had a feeling at the back of his mind that in it lay some connection with the case, that there at least he might find some of the answers to the questions which had started up in his mind when Gwen Bainbridge had spoken about her sister's marriage. He decided now was as good an opportunity as any of looking it over. He left the car in the car park and walked across.

Chapter eleven

If it were possible to concentrate all your efforts on one particular case, to the exclusion of all the rest, mused George Atkins, running his hand through his grizzled hair and ensuring himself a period of undisturbed privacy by lighting up his noxious pipe, life would be a darned sight easier—but when had it ever been? Just now the DCI needed all the men he could get on the Marion Dove case, but everything else couldn't be ignored. He pondered in particular the problem of this girl, this fifteen-year-old who'd gone missing while her parents had been on holiday abroad. He sat down, shuffled a few names and allocated jobs and in the end, not without some trepidation, he sent Deeley to see what he could get out of the friend who'd supposedly been staying with her during the absence of the parents, whom Atkins had already interviewed himself, and of whom he hadn't formed a very high opinion.

Nicola Parkin was, fortunately for Deeley, away from school with a cold, though when he was confronted with her, he could see no signs of it.

She was a tall, etiolated fifteen-year-old, blonde, and so thin as to be almost anorexic, and her voice was scarcely more than a whisper, so that Deeley had to strain to hear what she was saying. Her mother, on the other hand, had a loud and hectoring voice, to match her presence. So far she'd done most of the talking. Deeley let her run on, waiting patiently for the time when in the nature of things she must pause for breath. Nicola, it seemed, was in disgrace, but it was "that Katie Lazenby" who was bearing the brunt of Mrs. Parkin's wrath.

"I never did trust her, really. Sly, she is, I always said so—"

"Oh, Mum!" breathed Nicola.

"Oh yes I did, always. Involving my daughter in her lying and

scheming, how dare she! And you—" turning to her daughter
"—I shall have something to say to you, my girl, about all that,
just now, don't think you'll get away with it, telling lies just so
she could carry on and get up to God knows what while her
parents were out of the way! And what about her mother?" she
demanded of Deeley. "Disgusting I call it, willing to leave two
young girls on their own while they gad off abroad—Acapulco,
wasn't it?"

"The Algarve, Mum."

"Well, wherever. And not even taking the trouble to check
with me that I was agreeable. As if I would've been! Her Dad'll
have something to say about that, I can tell you. My Nicola, and
all my children, have been brought up right!"

"Mrs. Parkin, do you think I could trouble you for a drink?"
Deeley asked at last in desperation. "I've got a real thirst on."
The three of them, in that little sitting room, with the large
three-piece suite and the enormous TV set and music centre
dominating one side of it, seemed to take up a lot of air.

She looked at him sharply, but he was indeed looking warm.
"Go get the policeman a glass of water, Nicola," she ordered
and Deeley, mortified, saw that his ploy hadn't succeeded. He
wasn't going to get a cup of tea, as he'd hoped, and he wasn't
going to get Mrs. Parkin out of the room, either. She talked all
the time her daughter was absent, which seemed an inordinately
long time. Eventually, Nicola came back and handed him the
glass of water, then folded herself like an Anglepoise lamp and
sat down. Deeley took a long swig and said firmly, "Mrs. Parkin, I'd like to hear Nicola's own account of what's happened,
now, if you don't mind."

Nicola shrank further into the corner of the settee, her
mother crossed her arms over her militant bosom and tightened
her lips, looking offended. "Well, I don't know what more she
can tell you than I've done, I'm sure."

It took more patience than Deeley knew he possessed to get a
coherent story out of Nicola, who was terrified at what she'd
done, and more to prevent her formidable mother from interfering, but eventually Deeley's notes were complete and, as it
turned out, a good deal more relevant than anyone might have
thought.

He was chuffed. This'd bring a bit of colour to the DCI's cheeks.

After he left the glassworks, not quite knowing what to expect at The Mount, Mayo made his way up the drive between craggy stone rockeries dankly overhung with evergreens.

It was as Gwen Bainbridge had suggested, fixed in a time warp, an old dinosaur of a house. He wasn't averse to Victorian architecture; at its best he admitted it could be magnificent, but this was a different matter. Over-ornate for its size and proportions, The Mount was ugly by any standards. Constructed of dull red brick with string courses of yellow stone like marzipan in a simnel cake, with its steeply sloping grey slate roofs and tall chimneys and unnecessary turrets it had a slightly top-heavy look, as though too high for its base, as though a good push from behind would send it toppling into the neglected garden.

Before going into the house, he took stock of the surroundings, walking round the trodden and moss-grown red gravel path that circled the lawn, gingerly pushing aside the long, rampant tentacles of climbing roses which had long since blown away from the supports of their metal arches.

This had once been a fine garden but now the earth was sad and heavy, uncultivated beneath the unpruned shrubs. A lovely Victorian oval lead pond was choked with weeds and almost obscured by a small thicket of seedlings from the weeping ash at the corner of the path. Someone had carelessly rough-cut the lawn fairly recently, leaving long grass high between the swathes of the mower and at the lawn edges where old blue bricks set diagonally upright made a broken picot edge. Pigeons had roosted in the crannies and gullies of the angled roofs and behind the chimney stacks, and evidence of their presence was all around. Stepping carefully towards the massive front door, he put the key into the lock with some feeling of anticipation, instinctively ducking as an alarmed clatter of wings sounded and two pigeons swooped down and away.

Inside was a museum, furniture and fittings circa 1880. Ornate dark marble fireplaces with heavy overmantels, elaborate plaster ceilings and tall windows, leather and plush-covered armchairs and sofas, a smell of dust. Mrs. Bainbridge had exaggerated, but not much, in saying nothing had been allowed to change. There were a few later, obviously replacement furnishings here and there, anachronisms which did nothing to relieve the prevailing ambience of overall gloom. He walked in growing wonder from room to room—seven bedrooms, attics, one amazing, unbelievable bathroom. A huge drawing-room, a sombre dining-room off which led a sunless conservatory, a study, a depressing kitchen and sculleries and—the only pleasant room in the house—what he took to be a breakfast room of sorts. He was upstairs in one of the main bedrooms when he heard the sound of wheels on the gravel.

Walking swiftly to the window, he stood to one side, screened by dark green chenille curtains and a layer of yellowed lace, watching the small silver Peugeot climb the drive. The car drew to a halt beside the front door but no one alighted for some time. He waited patiently and presently a young woman got out, slamming the door behind her.

She stood for a moment facing the garden and then turned abruptly to the house and stopped, her figure foreshortened from his angle of perception, her hands thrust into the pockets of her denim skirt. Slowly then she walked towards the door and let herself in.

She'd been fooling herself to think it would be any different, that there would be no stifling sense of suffocation, that the grim, dimly lit hall where ghosts and witches had lurked in the shadows where she was a child on her way to bed would have been mysteriously lightened, that the pounding of her heart would be any less painful now than it had been then. Only now she couldn't, once the drawing-room door had closed behind them, grasp Shirley's hand tight as they raced up the stairs together. Even Shirley must have felt fear at times, pretend as she might.

She forced herself to walk through rooms she hadn't entered for ten years and more, while memory rushed back. The vast Victorian Gothic furniture in carved black oak, the oppressive wallpapers, Turkey carpets and heavy dark velvet hangings, the thick lace curtains—some of her friends would have drooled over its authenticity, the furnishings alone were going to be worth a fortune, but Rachel could only regard it with loathing. For a long time she stood looking at the leather wing chair that only her father had been allowed to occupy, still standing in front of the big mahogany desk in his study. Without looking at the portrait of him that hung over the mantel, she walked quickly out to the hall.

Her footsteps rang on the cold Minton-tiled floor and so familiar was its pattern of tans, blues and reds, with a black and white chequerboard edging, that she could have drawn it with her eyes shut. She halted at the foot of the oak staircase, the murky colours of the big mournful stained glass window on the half-landing obscuring what light there was, feeling again the deep chill that the vast old-fashioned radiators could never dispel seeping into her bones, seeing the iron grating on the floor where the wavering heat from the hot pipes came through and the fluff and grit went in . . . how could her mother have *endured* it?

Utter dejection swept her, she stood there without moving, consumed by it, weeping inwardly for Marion. Had there ever been happiness in this house, or laughter? There must have been, once. Children had lived here—and children and unrelieved gloom and misery were a contradiction in terms.

She lifted her head and her eyes lit on the mounted antlers halfway up the staircase upon which, on the day she left school, Shirley had irreverently and joyously thrown and impaled her school hat. For the first time since entering the house, her misery lifted a little.

Mayo heard her moving from room to room downstairs and then into the hall. As he came out of the bedroom and on to the galleried landing, his footsteps muffled by thick carpets, he could see her at the foot of the stairs, her head bowed, clasping the newel post with her forehead against the cold marble of the ball that surmounted it. Her unhappiness was so evident that to disturb her now would be an unpardonable intrusion and he moved swiftly and silently back into the bedroom, gave it a few minutes and then walked out again, this time making enough noise to warn her of his presence.

"Miss Dove?" he said, coming down the stairs. "Detective Chief Inspector Mayo, Lavenstock CID."

She waited for him, showing no surprise. "My sister told me she'd given you a key."

She accepted his condolences gravely, but with no trace of the grieving young woman he had glimpsed from upstairs. Her voice was quick and decisive and her handshake firm, though her fingers were icy cold and she was exceedingly pale. There was a strong resemblance between the two sisters but she was fairer and more sturdily built than Shirley Dainty and had that calm direct gaze of her mother's that had been his most lasting impression of her.

"I suppose you want to talk to me? Then if you've seen all you want, I'd prefer to go outside. This place hasn't changed. It still has all the welcome of a morgue." She caught her breath slightly, and as if her unfortunate choice of words could be exorcised by movement, walked rapidly out of the door, slamming it when he had followed her outside. "I can understand my mother walking out after my father died, not wanting to have anything to do with it ever again, even the business of selling it."

He'd have preferred to be able to watch the expressions on her face, to see if they echoed the uncompromising tones; it was difficult, pacing awkwardly side by side on the gravel and he was looking around for a seat of some kind when she said suddenly, "I don't know about you, but I could do with a cup of tea. I wonder if Hawley's are still in business? Shall we walk down and see?"

"That sounds like a good idea." He was awash with tea at the moment but willing to suffer if it would help to elicit information.

The steeply descending road that led past the glassworks at the side of the house and thence to the Lavenstock bypass had never been designed for the heavy traffic it now took. They had to wait several minutes, nearly asphyxiated by the hot smell of tarmac, dust and petrol, while a stream of container lorries and tankers thundered past and a space finally occurred which allowed them to cross. When they got there they discovered to her obvious satisfaction that the small baker's with its half dozen little chequered-cloth tables set out towards the back of the shop was still in the business of serving teas and home-made cakes. He ordered tea for two and it was brought almost immediately with scones and a selection of cakes.

She filled their cups from a large brown teapot and selected a slice of chocolate cake from the plate he offered. "I shall no doubt regret this later," she remarked, as she proceeded to eat it slowly and with serious concentration. "Shirley will have cooked an elaborate meal and if I don't do it justice she'll get all uptight and think it's not good enough, but there are times when something sweet is necessary, don't you agree? Echoes of the nursery?"

"Or something to do with the blood sugar, I suppose."

They sat in a small oasis of privacy among the other unoccupied tables, the only seated customers at that moment. It was nearly five o'clock and the women of Holden Hill who weren't still at work would be at home giving children their tea, preparing an evening meal. Mayo ate his scone and drank his tea while customers came in and bought from the counter sweet-smelling brown loaves and the meat pasties for which Rachel told him the shop was famed. Outside the heavy traffic continued to roar by.

"Thank you for being patient," she said presently. "I feel better now." But she'd pushed away her plate and he noticed she'd eaten barely a third of the cake. A little colour had come into her cheeks. Her hair had fallen forward, making her seem less strained.

"I'd like to talk to you about your mother, though it's more a matter of background than anything, since you weren't here at the weekend."

"Wasn't I? Who told you that?" The glance she gave him was sharp and speculative, and somewhat impatiently she told him she'd driven down on Sunday morning, because her mother had rung and said she'd like to see her rather urgently before she went on holiday. "She wouldn't say what it was over the telephone, but she sounded concerned, and as I was due to leave tomorrow to spend three weeks in Florence I came down straight away."

"What was it she wanted to see you about?"

The impatience drained away and a sadness settled on her face. "This is going to be difficult." She stared down at the chequered pattern of the tablecloth, as if she might find help and guidance there. When she eventually spoke her voice was husky, yet controlled. "She'd recently been told she didn't have long to live, and she wanted to talk to me. She—she thought I ought to know, in case anything happened while I was away . . ." She broke off. "Stupid of me, the post-mortem. I see you know that already?"

"Yes. I'm sorry. That was all your mother wanted to see you about?"

"What else?" she shrugged, but suddenly wary it seemed to him.

"Are you sure?"

He thought she might have been going to add something but she didn't.

"What time did you leave her?"

"I started out early and arrived somewhere around half past nine, and left about—oh, about half past eleven, because I knew she usually had lunch with my Aunt Gwen on Sundays. I'd have driven her up there but I had to get back."

So—if Rachel Dove had left her mother at eleven-thirty, and she had been dead by the time Gwen Bainbridge rang at one-thirty, this further reduced the time during which she might have met her death. In broad daylight? With someone coming to walk their dog, say, liable to pass by at any moment? Quite possible. A spur of the moment killing, which could have taken less than a minute, another minute to pitch her into the canal. But equally, there might have been another reason why she hadn't answered the telephone. He thought of the supermarket receipt, and the name Steven. And the time, 10.30, which wouldn't fit.

"Did she ever mention anyone called Steven?"

"Not that I remember. Someone up at the works, perhaps?" she said vaguely. "She promised she'd rest after I'd gone. She looked exhausted, and I felt guilty that I'd kept her talking so long. We'd talked, perhaps too much, about things that ought to have been said years ago . . ." She pushed her hair back behind her ears. Her face had become pinched and plain again. "We were at cross purposes, as usual."

"Cross purposes?"

"What I mean is, I was frantically upset at the news and I wanted her to let me arrange for her to have some sort of care. At the same time she was trying to persuade me not to cancel my holiday. She pointed out I couldn't do anything if I stayed and that she'd no intention of leaving the lockhouse until she had to."

He wondered why then Marion Dove had chosen this particular moment to tell her daughter such a thing, if she hadn't wanted her to cancel her holiday. Telling her could have served no useful purpose, surely, other than ruining the holiday for her. The sudden shock of hearing of her mother's death would have been no worse than worrying it might happen while she was away. There was more to it.

"Did you know she intended changing her will?"

It took her some time to consider her answer, but in the end she said yes, her mother had told her that.

"Did she tell you how?"

She stirred the dregs of her tea unnecessarily. "No. Except that it wasn't going to affect me."

Mayo didn't believe her. He was sure her mother *had* told her, and that for reasons of her own Rachel was being less than frank about revealing what it was. He decided, because he believed she was on the point of telling him other things and he didn't want to lose her, to let the lie pass for the moment . . . but he'd come back to it.

"I gave up arguing in the end, about her leaving. You couldn't ever persuade my mother into something she didn't want to do, and anyway, I believe she was happier down there at the Jubilee than she'd ever been. It seemed to me that if that was her wish, if she wanted to stay there right up to the end then no-one else had the right to make her choice for her—though my sister didn't entirely agree with me over this."

He could imagine that.

She said suddenly, almost as if she couldn't help herself, "My mother had a rotten life, you know, with my father. He was a violent man and I hated him. Not that it matters now, I don't suppose. It was all pretty sordid, but he's dead, she'd dead, it's all done with." After a bleak pause, she added, "No, that's never true, is it? The past always has a bearing on the present . . . I for one can never forget it, as for Shirley . . ."

"Well, anyway . . ." Her mind had shifted back from some disturbing thought and as she went on, it wasn't about her sister. "The truth is, they had rows, he and my mother, when he'd beat her up. He was careful never to give her a black eye or anything that could be seen, except he once attacked her with a knife. She had a huge gash across the back of her hand—she said she'd done it herself, cutting bread, but I never believed it. It's a fallacy to think it's only drunken labourers who beat up their wives, isn't it? I simply could not understand why she wouldn't leave him. No-one *has* to endure *that!*"

Indeed they did not. But the reasons why so many women did, and allowed themselves to be battered again and again by their men were complex and often defied understanding.

Financial dependency, he suggested, especially when there were children—

"She could have got a job. She was more than competent." Her lips tightened, and she frowned. Remembered anger was competing with distress and anger won. "I've tried to understand why he needed to be like that, and believe me, I know all the fashionable excuses . . . frustration, low self-esteem, insecurity about his masculinity. Or just that maybe *his* father beat his mother. Violence creates violence, that's the current thinking, isn't it, that brutality is inherited? Do you think that's true? Do you think it's in the blood?" She shot the question at him as if he were one of her students.

"No," he said, though his views were not as rigid as that. But it was what she needed to hear, and it saved him from the sort of digressive discussion he'd no desire to get involved in at the moment. "What did they quarrel about?"

There was a moment of silence before she answered. "I think it was mostly about us, Shirley and me. He was disappointed in having daughters instead of sons for his precious business. If he'd had more wit to see it, he could have trained us to carry it on, but I don't suppose that ever occurred to him—that a woman could ever do a thing like that—he'd have been amazed to see how my mother ran the business after he died—much better than he ever did."

"Did he ever use violence against you and your sister?"

A lorry, crashing its gears on the hill outside, provided time for her to think. Her answer was cautious. "Occasionally, when we were children, though never if my mother was there, and only once later, in my case. I see—I believe now, because of what she told me—that he was afraid of us."

She was watching him warily, waiting for him to ask what she meant, but he had no need, he knew, immediately. "Afraid of you?" he nevertheless asked, more gently than he'd replied to her other question.

"He had a fancy, my father, for young girls. Under age to be precise, fourteen or fifteen." He saw the effort it had cost her to tell him. He thought he understood also now, only too well, that moment of despair at the bottom of the staircase, but softly she added, so softly he had to strain to hear, "No, he never touched us, he wouldn't have dared. My mother knew too much about him, you see." Then looking at him with that clear, direct gaze of her mother, she asked, "Are you shocked?"

"I've been a policeman too long for that, Miss Dove."

Not shocked—but some things could still sicken him. What he thought must have showed on his face.

"She tried to make me see on Sunday that he wasn't really evil, just weak and insecure. Oh, I daresay he *had* a pretty low self-esteem, which isn't surprising, considering everything. But it didn't make me feel one jot differently about him. I still feel he was a bastard, hard as nails, but soft and rotten at the core."

Despite the harshness of her judgement, some of the bitterness seemed to have drained out of her. She said, as if she were suddenly very tired, "I think she was sorry for him in a way, but that wasn't the real reason why she'd stayed with him. She didn't care about money, not for its own sake, not for herself . . . that was something we *were* agreed on. Money doesn't matter greatly to me, either. But her attitude was she'd brought us into the world and it was up to her to provide for us as best she could. What an inheritance!"

"Thank you for telling me." It couldn't have been easy. Even Gwen Bainbridge, who had very nearly told him, yesterday, hadn't quite been able to bring herself to do so.

"Thank *you* for the tea, I must be going now." She pushed her chair back and said with a difficult smile, "This is something I've never, ever mentioned to anyone. I don't know why I have now. You're very easy to confide in."

He grinned to himself, thinking what Kite and a few others would have said if they'd heard that. He didn't actually believe it himself in any case. It was simply that he'd been there, available, at a vulnerable and unguarded moment when she had felt it possible to unburden herself of years of inhibition. He had the impression she was glad that she had spoken, however, that a long-borne burden had been eased a little from her shoulders. He sat for several minutes more after she had left him, thinking over what she'd said. It might well turn out to have a bearing on the case. He would need to see her again, when the pattern had emerged more clearly. And the next time, he wouldn't let her get away with less than the truth.

Chapter twelve

When he heard what Atkins and Deeley wanted to see him about, Mayo sent for Kite and had them all three come up to his office. Kite, who had spent all afternoon checking through the interviews with the various people Ken Dainty had produced to support his alibi, and felt he could do with a change of direction, came in with alacrity, just behind the other two.

Mayo waved them all to sit down and perched himself on the edge of the desk. "All right, let's have it right from the beginning."

Atkins began with his own account of seeing the parents of Katie Lazenby after they'd discovered their daughter missing on their arrival home from holiday, three days earlier than expected. "Didn't come up to scratch, I gather, the Algarve, so they packed it in."

It appeared that the only time they'd been able to get a suitable booking was when Katie was back at school after the holidays, and so they'd arranged for the grandmother to stay with her. However, just before they were due to go, the old lady had broken her hip in a fall and had been in hospital ever since. Young Katie had pestered her parents not to cancel their holiday and to be allowed to stay on her own. Eventually they'd agreed, on condition that she had her friend, Nicola Parkin, to stay with her.

Deeley, who had taken his notebook out to make sure of getting his facts straight, took up his part of the story eagerly. "Nicola told Mrs. Lazenby she'd asked her mother's permission, and got it—which wasn't true of course, sir."

"Didn't Mrs. Lazenby check?"

"Apparently not, she just took Nicola's word."

"Shouldn't think, from what I saw of her," Atkins intervened, "she'd bother much with that sort of thing, in case it interfered with her own plans. And of course Nicola had no need to mention it to her mother, because there was never any intention of her going to stay with Katie—that was all malarkey, just a blind. She'd other fish to fry, young Katie. Sounds a right little madam, if you ask me."

"She was making use of Nicola, sir," Deeley said. "The poor kid's frightened to death at what she's done, incidentally."

"And so she should be. What made her agree to it?"

"Seems this Katie's one of the clever ones at school, shines at everything, and she agreed to help Nicola, who's always in trouble with her maths, if she'd do as she asked."

"And why was she so anxious to be alone?" Mayo asked, wearily, because he knew the answer that was coming and didn't want to hear it. Another precocious child, prepared to jeopardise her future, mess up her life—there'd be a boy in it somewhere, no doubt . . . and then knew where it was all leading, and why Deeley was so excited. "Paul Fish?" he asked softly.

"That's right, sir. Seems he's been soft on her for months, but she's kept him on a string, made him pretty miserable with it, and then suddenly she gives in and they start going out with one another . . ."

So there could now be an entirely different reason for Paul's abrupt departure from the scene, a much more acceptable one. What, after all, was the hard evidence against him regarding Marion Dove? Nothing but speculation. On the other hand, it seemed fairly conclusive that Paul *had* taken Gwen Bainbridge's car—not to mention her Visa card—and that was more in line with the sort of thing a boy might do if he was setting out to impress a girl and needed money. Five hundred pounds in cash, of course, the missing five hundred, would have been even more useful.

"What d'you think, Martin?" he asked when the other two had gone.

"I'd put money on it that Paul was just fed up after the row with his father and decided to push off, probably only for a few days until he'd cooled off, taking Katie with him, know what I mean?"

"I do know what you mean. But—robbing his aunt of the five hundred pounds to finance the jaunt? Having first murdered her? If he did, it would have meant him going about his business for the rest of the day as if nothing had happened, even to ferrying Mrs. Bainbridge about, only deciding to decamp either very late that night or early the next morning. Which seems pretty cool—and indicates a certain complicity on the part of Katie Lazenby." Mayo shook his head. "Possible, of course, but probable? I don't know. I just don't know."

He liked Alex in uniform. She was one of the few women who could wear it without looking either lumpy or butch. But he preferred her as she was tonight. She'd been dozing in front of the television when he rang the bell, relaxed in a dark blue shirt in some silky material and a longish sort of skirt that drifted as she walked, and her hair was a little tousled where her head had rested on the cushion, her cheeks flushed with sleep.

After all these months, he still felt it necessary to apologize for arriving without warning but she welcomed him as if his unexpected appearance was the most agreeable thing that had happened to her all week. That was one of the best things about her —her readiness and ability to understand the haphazard irregularity of his life without fuss, to provide a warm and loving atmosphere with no hassle. The other side of the coin was that Mayo wanted to be married and Alex didn't. He told himself in moments of trying to understand her point of view it was simply that he wanted a hand to hold, a presence in the dark, someone in the other chair. Maybe. But whatever it was, he wanted it permanent, and because she was wary of anything less than a perfect relationship, and saw that there were reasons on both sides why this might never be possible, she preferred, insisted on remaining uncommitted.

"You look bushed, Gil. I'm afraid I've already eaten, but I can do you a couple of lamb chops. Will that do?"

"Fine." They'd be perfect, too. She was incapable of doing anything less than excellently. All very well, but she tended to have the same expectations of others. It was a nagging fact that occasionally disquieted the corners of his mind when he was trying to persuade her that she couldn't have her cake and eat it. Which was how he saw it, but she didn't.

"Get yourself a drink while you're waiting."

He followed her into the small kitchen, helped himself to a beer and hitched a hip on to the edge of the table, watching her while she moved efficiently around, admiring her back view, the tall slimness of her. "Any leads yet?" she asked over her shoulder, taking salad from the fridge.

Briefly, he brought her up to date with what had happened, the latest about Paul Fish.

The chops, succulent and pink inside, exactly as he liked them, arrived on the table, magically accompanied by a crisp salad, a couple of warm rolls and butter and a pot of strong dark coffee. She poured herself a cup and sat opposite while he ate. "What do these wretched parents expect, for heaven's sake? Leaving a girl that age?" she commented. But she seemed to sense that he didn't want to talk about the case, that tonight he wanted to switch off, and while he ate they talked about his holiday, or rather he talked and she listened.

"It sounds marvellous!"

For a moment, he regretted not having asked her to accompany him to Scotland, but when he tried to imagine her struggling across the boggy moors in a drenching Scottish mist, he failed. Her dark blue skirt exactly matched the dark blue of her shirt, which exactly matched the blue of her eyes. Her nails were short and very clean, polished to pale, pearly pink ovals. Yet he knew how tough she was, she knew how to take care of herself in a rough-house, she knew what was what, having done her share of the rotten, sometimes unspeakable jobs, like any other police officer, man or woman.

He really enjoyed the food, finding himself more hungry than he'd known he was. "This is good, love. The two women in my life, both super cooks—what have I done to deserve that?"

He saw immediately that she didn't altogether like that, that for some reason he'd said the wrong thing, but couldn't for the life of him see why. Sometimes he felt that conversation with Alex was like stepping through a minefield. You never knew what you were going to put your foot on next. She could be acid about remarks he considered quite innocent, but this seemed to apply to ninety percent of women these days.

His meal finished, they went back into her sitting room. She put on a new record she'd bought, a collection of Scarlatti harpsichord sonatas. He suspected, because their tastes in music rarely coincided, that she'd bought the record especially because she knew he liked it, and was touched.

She'd created a lovely restful room, decorated in the cool, neutral colours she loved, resisting the blandishments of her sister to reconstruct and reproduce a facsimile of the apartment's elegant Edwardian past. Lois, who ran a swish interior decorator's business from a shop in the town, and thought nothing of redoing a room entirely, throwing out everything else simply on account of some new chair or cabinet, or even a picture she'd bought, thought it a chance wasted, but Alex liked and kept the things she'd collected over the years, and with them had achieved an elegance of her own.

She hadn't drawn the curtains across the open window and framed between their lavender grey velvet folds he could see the three-dimensional tracery of leaves and branches of one of the trees in the park opposite, lit by the street lamp, a blurred, grainy light emphasising the darkness beyond. The jungle outside the territory of the campfire, where in the night lurked lawlessness, the unknown, terror and murder. "Tyger, tyger, burning bright, in the forests of the night . . ." Blake. Marion Dove.

She had liked poetry. These cool, precise Scarlatti cadences, or Mozart, Bach, Elgar, Prokofiev, none of them had probably meant a thing to her, but words forming patterns on the page had said something to her heart. He still didn't know what sort of woman she really was. She had been quiet and unassuming, leading a quiet uneventful life. An ordinary woman, with nothing so far revealed in her lifestyle or her make-up to lead anyone to murder her. Except for one thing.

She had had money, and the power that money brings. Had she been the sort to wield that power? To enjoy manipulating people, using her money as a lever? From what he had gathered, that seemed to be the last thing she would do. Her interest in money had seemingly been for her daughters only, but it had been strong enough to induce her to stay married to a man like Wesley Dove for more than twenty-five years.

But there had to be, somewhere, a reason for her having met so horrible, so sad a death. He had a strong ineluctable feeling that he ought to know, that he had already been told the facts that would lead him to his murderer. The facts were there, randomly distributed in his subconscious. It was a matter of looking at what there was to see, and seeing its relevance, but gathering

them together felt maddeningly beyond him tonight. And also,
his eyes kept straying to an opened envelope with a Bradford
postmark, propped on the mantelpiece, addressed to Alex in
stylish handwriting, cursive, thick and black.

Liam. He'd never seen this Liam's handwriting, the man on
whose account Alex had left Yorkshire and been transferred
down here, but he knew it was his. His handwriting *would* be
like that, fancy, the handwriting of an Irish Don Juan, flamboy-
ant, untrustworthy, a man who'd no intention of leaving his
wife, or letting Alex alone, either. He'd have smiling Irish eyes,
too, and that he had a great line in blarney was implicit in the
fact that she evidently couldn't, despite the way he'd treated her,
break entirely free.

He made an effort to empty his mind. He'd been at it fourteen hours on the trot . . . he heard the record come to an end
. . . The telephone rang, jerking him fully awake. Alex went
into the hall to answer it and after a few minutes' conversation,
during which he heard laughter, she came back and said, "It's
for you, it's Julie."

"Here?" He felt ridiculously guilty, and annoyed with himself for being so. Like many men, he was prudish as far as his
daughter was concerned; so far, he'd preferred not to think
about whether she'd correctly interpreted Alex's place in his
life. Whenever they met, Alex and Julie got along fine, they
seemed to understand each other very well. Sometimes, he had
a suspicion they were ganging up on him.

"Julie?" he said, cautiously.

"Hi, Dad! Hope you don't mind my ringing so late," she said
cheerfully. "I tried the flat and thought maybe Alex could give
you a message. I was just wondering, there's a concert in Leeds
we could go to after the do on Saturday, shall I book? Everything should be over by six at the latest and you won't want to
hang around talking to the relatives, will you?"

God, he thought, the wedding!

He said, "Julie, I'll do my best, but the chances are I shan't
make it, the wedding I mean. There's something come up—it's a
murder case, and I don't think there's a hope we shall be clear
by Saturday. I'm sorry."

She knew he'd forgotten. The slight pause before she answered was fractionally too long, it seemed to him, her voice

when she did answer was to his ears just too light and unconcerned. Thus, and thus, and thus, the pattern of his life with
Lynne. Or was he being over-sensitive? "I'm sorry as well, Dad,
but never mind—murder, that's important. Anyway, family
weddings aren't exactly your scene, are they?"

He wasn't sorry actually to have the best of excuses for getting out of it. He might approve of marriage, but with scornful
masculinity, he hated weddings, even the wedding of a favourite
niece, his sister's daughter. He was sorry, however, to rob Julie
of her good intentions. It had been a gentle thought.

His daughter was in the middle of her training in catering and
hotel management and had very definite ideas about one day
owning her own restaurant. As part of her course, she was doing
a stint in a hotel in Yorkshire, and had as a consequence been
seeing a lot of her northern relatives, and been involved in the
preparations for her cousin's wedding.

"Maybe it's not in my line, but I'd have been there if I could,
you know that. Isn't there a disco thing afterwards for the
younger end?"

"Yes, Dad, I'll stay on for that. I expect Aunt Isobel or someone will put me up. I'll make your excuses. And listen, don't
worry about it, I only thought, if you were going to be at a loose
end . . ."

Perhaps she wasn't feeling let down. Perhaps she was feeling
quite relieved, really, that she'd be free to enjoy herself with the
other young people. Perhaps it was only his own conscience,
and the echoes of Lynne, and the times he'd let her down, that
were bothering him.

"I'm really sorry, love, but I'll make my own excuses, thanks
all the same. Look, the next weekend you're free, come home
and we'll fix something up, right?"

"Right, Dad, I will, that'll be great."

If nothing else crops up, he thought, no more murder, arson,
robbery with violence, shoplifting, indecent exposure. He went
back to Scarlatti and his—Alex's—armchair, his peace of mind
thoroughly shattered.

As he picked up his whisky tumbler, he saw that the envelope
from Bradford had gone from the mantelpiece.

Chapter thirteen

It had rained during the night. The morning had a tranquil grey coolness, the hiatus of late summer before the smoky hazes of autumn came. Kite was wearing a jacket for the first time in weeks. Mayo strode into the office, restless, impatient, demanding feedback from Forensics, not yet through.

"I'll chase them up," Kite told him, "but you know what they'll say. They're convinced we expect miracles."

"And why not? A miracle's the only way we're going to get this job started, as I see it. And they've had two days, for God's sake! Never mind their tender feelings, you jump on them. Make 'em earn their keep."

And *he* was supposed to be the impatient one! Kite deemed it wiser not to say that two days was no time at all, even by Mayo's standards. For now, it was a case of collecting facts, questioning witnesses, checking alibis until sooner or later a clear suspect with a strong enough motive would emerge. Unless this turned out to be a mindless, motiveless killing—a thing far rarer than people imagined though, most murders being committed by people who knew their victim.

Kite was for once more tactful than Mayo had suggested, and as a result the forensic people were prepared to be helpful. Prints found in the house had belonged to the victim and to both her daughters; those on the chessmen corresponded with Mrs. Dove's and those of Paul Fish, taken from his room. There were none anywhere belonging to Ken Dainty. But—an unidentified set had been found on the gin bottle in the sideboard and the empty one in the dustbin.

And one other fact interested Mayo very much. At the spot where the body had been found, it was impossible to detect any footprints. At a little distance under the trees, however, were some deep indentations in the grass, not precise or easily identifiable because of the loose, stony nature of the soil, but consistent with, say, the high heel of a woman's shoe.

Marion Dove's white shoes, though fairly new and quite fashionable, had been low, almost flat heeled. She had not, apparently, possessed a pair of high-heeled shoes. There were three other women whom they had interviewed of course—but two of them were her daughters, the other her sister. Nevertheless . . .

"A woman?" Kite made a dubious face. Women were not notably stranglers. "That's a bizarre thought!" But he knew that the possibility, however unlikely or unwelcome, couldn't be dismissed. Nothing could, or indeed should be ruled out. It had been a straightforward strangulation, not, as such cases often were, accompanied by rape or sexual assault. Nor had any considerable strength been needed to kill her. Marion Dove, like Anne Boleyn, had had "a very little neck." A woman could easily have done it.

"Though at the moment, it's hard to see how or why." Mayo began to tick the women off on his fingers. "Gwen Bainbridge had had words with her. She's no spring chicken, admittedly, but she's far from decrepit. Also, she probably stands to gain from the will. Then there's Shirley Dainty—a neurotic woman, with an expensive lifestyle, and hiding something, if I'm not mistaken . . ."

"She has nails an inch long, and there were no nail-marks on the neck," Kite remarked.

"True," Mayo agreed. "And they can both account for the two hours in question—Mrs. Bainbridge cooking the roast pork and stuffing, Mrs. Dainty knocking back the G & Ts at the golf club. That leaves Rachel Dove. Of the three, she's the most problematic, the one with the best opportunity, and the least motive—if we can believe her claim not to be interested in money."

"Is anybody?" Kite asked cynically, as Farrar knocked and put his blond head round the door, looking alert and for some reason slightly amused.

"It looks as though things are hotting up, sir. We've got a witness downstairs—the woman who looks after the donkeys on the Compsall Road, a Miss Martha Witherspoon. She says she might have seen someone coming out of the lane on Sunday night."

"Might have seen?" Mayo repeated, following Farrar down the corridor. "Did she or didn't she?"

"Don't know, sir, she hasn't been properly questioned yet. The inspector thought you'd like to do that." Farrar was passing the overhead fan as he spoke, and it lifted the clutch of papers in his hand. Not a hair of his blond head moved. Does he use *hair spray?* wondered Mayo, fascinated.

The reason for Farrar's amusement became clear as soon as Mayo entered the room. Miss Witherspoon, Martha, wasn't in the least what he'd expected. Someone with a name like that who cared for superannuated donkeys had prepared him for a kind of dotty Margaret Rutherford look alike, not this tiny girl of about twenty or so with a slim, boyish figure and shining fair hair clasped at the side with a tortoiseshell slide, a face innocent of make up. Her jeans were pressed with a crease down the centre of the leg and her spanking white T-shirt showed an almost breastless figure. She was cradling a cup of tea, the thick white china looking too heavy for her two small hands to support as she drank in a series of delicate sips.

"Now, Miss Witherspoon," he began, feeling faintly foolish at using the inappropriate name.

"Marty," she said, with a shy smile. "Please call me Marty."

"I know you've already told Detective Sergeant Kite why you're here, er, Marty, but perhaps you wouldn't mind repeating it?"

"Oh no, not at all. Daddy warned me I should have to make a statement and I was quite prepared." Her voice was little-girl to match her appearance. She had the hint of a lisp and her face shone with cleanliness and earnestness. She sat well back in her chair, so that her feet in their red and white trainers scarcely touched the ground. He was already beginning to find her irritating. Mainly because she was much older than he'd first thought, he was almost sure nearer thirty than twenty, and he'd no patience with women who refused to keep pace with their age.

"We-ell . . . I go down to the Compsall Road twice a day to see to my animals, to give them food and water and things, once in the morning before I go to work—" He glanced at the particulars Farrar had taken down. Marty Witherspoon worked in the Midland Bank, and lived in one of the large Victorian houses in Park Road, not far from the house where Alex had her flat. "—and once in the evening. I was quite late finishing on Sunday, I have a newcomer to my little family and he's taking time to settle down, poor thing." The corners of her mouth turned down censoriously. "He wasn't well-treated in his previous home and—"

"Sunday *night,* you said. What time was this?" Mayo interrupted, fearing some diatribe on animal rights. "Do you remember?"

"Oh yes, I do, it was half-past nine. It was getting quite dark and I'd promised the parents I wouldn't be late . . . Daddy usually drives me down in the evening, but they had guests on Sunday."

"I see. So tell me what you saw."

"I was just padlocking the gate, and I saw this man come staggering out of the entrance to the lane . . . I mean, *reeling.* I shut my flashlight off and kept very quiet and just hoped he wouldn't see me. Daddy's always warning me to be careful when I go down there alone at night. I mean, the Dog and Fox is just along the road, and I assumed he'd probably come from there and was drunk."

"But you said he'd come from the lane."

"Oh yes, he had. But I expect he'd been—well, you know, if he'd come from the pub . . ." She wriggled in her chair and lowered her eyes modestly.

"You thought he'd been to obey a call of nature, Miss Witherspoon?" Mayo asked, despising the euphemism but resisting the temptation to be plainer.

"Mmm."

"Which direction did he take?"

"Towards Holden Hill."

"Would you recognise him again?"

"Oh no, I've told you it was quite dark and he was under the trees and he never turned his face towards me."

"How was he dressed?" She shook her head helplessly. "Tall or short, heavily built or slight? Did you get any impression of his age?"

"I really didn't notice. I got into my car rather quickly, you see, and drove off."

"You'd see him again in your headlights, then?"

"No, because I always go the other way, the way my car's facing, and circle back into the town. It's easier than trying to turn on the Compsall Road."

"Was there a vehicle of any sort parked nearby?"

"I—don't think so."

"But you can't be sure?"

"There wasn't when I left. There *may* have been one when I got there, there sometimes is, but I wouldn't like to swear to it . . . I'm sorry."

Her confidence was shaken. She looked so woebegone he told her not to worry, she'd been a great help. He thanked her for her public-spirited action in coming forward, he'd contact her again if necessary. She beamed, wriggled off the chair like a child, and trotted away.

The most likely explanation of what she'd seen was most probably the right one—some drunk staggering along from the Dog and Fox, rather than the murderer, unless the murder had taken place some considerable time later than had been thought. But by an association of ideas, he decided it wouldn't do any harm to find out where Charlie Fish had been at nine thirty on Sunday evening.

"That's a pleasure in store for you," he told Kite as they eventually set out to drive up to the glassworks, with Kite at the wheel. "But for now, get your skates on, Martin, I've got the inquest at half eleven and I don't want to rush this interview with Dainty."

Ken Dainty had barely had time to open his post that morning before Rachel was shown into his office.

"Come in, sit down."

He spoke without turning round, carefully closing and locking the two illuminated corner cabinets in the room, where the colours and lustrous textures of a magnificent collection of old glass glowed behind the panels of the doors. "Rustle up some coffee for us, will you, Val?" he asked, and only then did he give his full attention to his sister-in-law. "Well, what is it that's so important that you have to come down here for, Rachel? Couldn't you have seen me at home?"

"I've been trying to get you alone, ever since I came down. You were busy all day yesterday and we simply can't talk when Shirley's around, the way she is. I know she's upset, but so are we all, and refusing to discuss it isn't going to make things easier."

"Discuss what?"

"You know perfectly well what I mean. There isn't any need to pretend obtuseness with me. I've known you long enough to believe better of you than that. What are we going to tell the police about Sunday?"

"I thought we'd agreed on that, right from the first. We say nothing. That way, no-one will be wiser, no-one will be hurt."

"Ken, I've been in a state of shock ever since you rang me with the news. I wouldn't otherwise have agreed to anything so morally indefensible and ultimately futile. Legally obstructive too, I shouldn't wonder."

Ken gave a short bark of derisive laughter at the high-flown words, and she flushed as she realized how ridiculous she'd sounded. "Wouldn't you?" he said dryly. "You were there as well, remember?"

"I spoke with the Chief Inspector yesterday, as I told you. The only reason I didn't say anything then was because I thought she'd be—"

Oh God, you had to be so careful, not only in *what* you said to Shirley, but what you said *about* her, but really, it was high time all that pretence was stopped. Yesterday, and her talk with Mayo, had made her see that. She'd spent a sleepless night and felt physically wretched, but had come to the decision that the hoary old skeleton in the cupboard must be brought out into the light of day. Otherwise its grisly unseen presence was going to go on disrupting all their lives, not least her own—and Josh's. It saddened her that it had taken the horror of her mother's death and a talk with Mayo, a stranger, to show her how unfair she'd been in not telling Josh the truth and letting him make his own assessments, in not allowing him to help her. In admitting that she needed help. Was it, she thought with something approaching terror, too late? Too late for her, too late for Shirley? She wondered how much, if at all, Ken and Shirley had ever discussed the problem. Very little, she doubted, that was why they were in this mess.

At that moment, the coffee came in. When it had been served and they were alone once again she determined to grasp the opportunity. "She isn't very happy, is she, Ken?"

He didn't pretend this time not to understand who she meant. "Shirley wouldn't be happy if you gave her the moon and wrapped the stars up with it."

She sipped her coffee and watched him steadily. They'd never had much to say to one another, she and Shirley's husband, they operated on different wavelengths, but up to now she'd always respected him, and liked him well enough to be sorry at the change in him. He never used to be bitter. Poor Ken, who didn't try to be anything other than he was and didn't realize he was all the better for that. Who was, for all that, a dark horse.

He drained his coffee and looked pointedly at the clock on the wall. "If that's all you've got to say, you'd better go. I've got that detective inspector coming to see me in a few minutes."

"In that case *you* can tell him."

He ignored that, saying in his abrupt way, "I've had a phone call this morning."

"From—?"

"Yes."

"There you are, then. What if he tells them we were there?"

"Not he. He'll be putting himself right in it if he does, don't forget. We can all testify what went on between him and Marion."

"What did he want?"

"He says he wants what he was promised."

She said slowly, after a moment, "Why not? Don't we have a moral obligation? My mother *did* intend him having something, after all. It was only his attitude that made her so reluctant to say so definitely. That—and what you'd told her, I suppose. She was always like that—if you tried to push her, she dug her heels in all the more."

His head had jerked up and he stared at her in uncomprehending silence as she spoke. He thought how plain she looked this morning, colourless. She'd always been one whose looks depended on her moods and feelings. When she was happy, she was lit up, and looked nearly beautiful. Today the lamp burned very low, she was turned right down. He'd heard Shirley say there was a man, up there at Northumbria. Well, good luck to him! Rachel wasn't a gift he'd wish on anybody. "Like hell we will," he said. "And aren't you forgetting something? What if he killed her?"

"Did he, though? Did he, Ken?" Her steady, unwavering gaze fixed itself on his face, his truculent pose across the desk, arms folded, head lowered, like an angry bull looking over a fence.

"I'm not sure I understand what you're getting at," he said, dangerously quiet. "What's that supposed to mean?"

"Well, don't let's pretend you wouldn't do just about *anything* for your old glassworks, shall we?" she said, suddenly hostile, moving her arm in a sweeping gesture that encompassed the yard outside and the glowing cabinets in the corner, and five hundred years of family history, pride and arrogance. "What you did to my mother—that was cruel, and it proves what I mean. It's an obsession with you, just as it became an obsession with her. It seems you get like that when you marry into this family."

His face was suffused with temper. "That is so bloody stupid," he said, enunciating each word carefully, "it doesn't need an answer."

Her own anger flared up. "The whole thing's stupid! We should have told the truth in the first place. I'm supposed to be making a signed statement to the police, and I'm certainly not prepared to put my name to a load of downright lies. I shall tell them he was there."

"Don't do that," he said, his voice suddenly cold. "Not before you think a lot more carefully about it. If we start changing our story now, they'll think we really have got something to hide. We say nothing. You say not one word, is that clear? Right, then—end of story."

Chapter fourteen

Half-running across the car park towards a silver Peugeot in the far corner when they arrived at Dove's Glass was a woman Mayo instantly recognised as Rachel Dove.

"That's her—the younger daughter I saw yesterday at The Mount!"

They followed her progress with interest, a young woman obviously in a fair old temper. A hundred yards of car park couldn't disguise the fury. It seemed Rachel Dove might have inherited her mother's level gaze but not her calm temperament. The set of her head and shoulders showed it, the swift angry flick of her skirt as she got into the driving seat, the quick reverse and the speed with which she shot out of the car park. Mayo wasn't sure whether she'd noticed their car or not, but it didn't matter. He wasn't yet ready to see her again.

They found Kenneth Dainty dusting the contents of the top shelf of a tall, illuminated glass-fronted cabinet, one of two in the corners of his office. He greeted them with a faintly embarrassed nod and a quick excuse for the duster in his hand. "Won't be long. Always see to this myself, you have to take it slow, see. Just the job for lowering the blood pressure, they tell me."

"Please carry on, we're in no particular hurry." Not true at all, but truth was an expendable commodity in the interests of achieving cooperation, which might not, in the circumstances, be easy, if Rachel Dove had left Dainty in a condition where he needed calming down—which might well be the case. Mayo had an idea that she could be a very unsettling young woman if she chose.

It *was* Dainty she'd been to see. On his desk were two empty coffee cups. The air held a faint evocation of the scent she used, sophisticated yet romantic, sharp, with hints of rose: a surprising choice, though perhaps someone else had chosen it for her, someone who knew her better than she knew herself.

It was hard to tell whether the anger he'd sensed in her was reciprocated in Ken Dainty. His appearance was much as it had been the only other time Mayo had seen him, tough, uncommunicative, facing the world with his own brand of head-down truculence, frowning with concentration as he completed his task.

"You've a pretty good collection of glass there, Mr. Dainty."

"Not bad, I suppose." But Dainty's expression lightened. "You interested?"

Mayo nodded. He was moderately interested in the glass, but more intrigued by the way the big man's hands almost caressed each fragile object as he replaced it precisely. "What are these little things here?"

"You'll very likely have seen them in the local antique shops, sir," Kite offered.

"And ridiculous prices they ask for them, too!" Dainty intervened.

"I knew an old man used to work here and he'd make them for us when we were kids. Aren't they called friggers, Mr. Dainty?"

"That's right, they are." They were apprentice pieces, he explained, or bits of spare-time nonsense, made from waste glass. "Blown scores myself, in my time," he said. But he reckoned most of those in the cabinet went back further than that. They were charming little specimens of the glassmaker's art, objects ranging through minute replicas of umbrellas, swans, a pair of tiny bellows and a miniature pump, complete with bucket, to a fully rigged sailing ship. He didn't trust them into his audience's hands, doubtless believing, quite wrongly, they wouldn't exercise the necessary care, not knowing Mayo's expertise with the tiniest of watch and clock parts.

"If you want to see something really old, though, take a look at these." He opened the twin cabinet in the opposite corner, and began to explain with mounting enthusiasm the various pieces of glass and their origins—Rhenish and Bohemian glass, English flintglass, beakers and rummers, posset pots and goblets, greenish bottles made iridescent by time and weather, enamelled and cameo glass, soda glass, cranberry and Bristol opaque . . ." He brought himself up short. "Sorry, once you start collecting it gets you, like a virus."

Mayo waved a deprecatory hand. "Worth a fair amount, I expect?"

"Can't say I've ever totted it up, but likely it's worth a bob or two. But if you're talking of *value* . . . this is what you should be looking at. Not in money terms maybe, but there's other sorts. It's only a fragment broken off one of the pots used to melt the glass—if you look, you can still see some of the vitrified metal on the side—but it must be about four or five hundred years old. It came from one of the original furnaces in the Darney Forest in Lorraine."

He picked up, and this time handed to Mayo, what looked like nothing more than a piece of jagged grey rock but was really, he explained, a lump of grainy rock-hard clay to which was bonded an eighth of an inch layer of glass, translucent, blu-ish-green, the colour of sea water.

"They were making this sort of glass as far back as the fif-teenth century, and before, our ancestors over there. There was a mystique about making glass in those days—and a lot of super-stition. Folks thought it was black magic, but I don't suppose the old lads cared, why should they? They were gentlemen glass-makers, they owned lands and property, they had titles to their name. All had to be left behind, of course."

"What brought them over here?"

"Oh, religious persecution among other things." They had been Huguenots, he said, and had come to England at the royal request of Queen Elizabeth, to revive her dying glass industry, first to the Sussex Weald, then later, when they had been forced to start using coal for their furnaces, to Stourbridge. At that time they'd been mainly manufacturers of broadglass, made by blow-ing a big cylinder of glass metal and then splitting it open to form a square which was afterwards cut into quarries—the little squares seen in old lattice windows. "I'm a practical glassmaker myself and I can tell you that must have been heavy work, swinging and working a hot bulb of molten glass weighing sev-eral pounds . . ." Dainty stopped abruptly, the animation leav-ing his face. "I'm talking too much. Glassmaking's been my life, I get carried away."

"No, no, please go on." By this time Mayo's curiosity was

aroused. It was a fallacy, he thought, to believe that people were necessarily boring when they talked shop—especially when it was their all-consuming passion. He'd known otherwise dull and tedious people suddenly become fascinating when speaking of what was overridingly important to them. It was enlightening to have seen what motivated this man, what might release that controlled force one could sense just under the surface. He could see Kite also looking at Dainty with speculative interest, and wondered if he too, had noticed how the other man had spoken of "our" ancestors, quite unselfconsciously. Meaning perhaps the whole race of glassmakers, or simply the Dove family, with whom he had apparently so wholeheartedly identified himself? Whichever, passion had been there when he spoke and when he handled the glass, and where there is passion, there is single-mindedness, often a refusal to admit any other point of view, sometimes a ruthlessness in achieving the desired object, Mayo thought.

"On the contrary," he said, "you've whetted my appetite. I'd like to see the manufacturing process some time, if that's possible."

But Dainty evidently felt he had said too much already, seeming even slightly ashamed to have let himself show any emotion. He'd switched off again, or rather switched back to the self he chose to project. "I'll get someone to show you round, just let me know when you're ready," he said abruptly. "Though we don't make anything very fancy nowadays. We have our lines, top-quality lead crystal with mostly traditional patterns, and we stick to them. Run-of-the-mill stuff." He waved them to a couple of seats. "I've wasted enough of your time. What did you want to see me about?" Assuming what is generally regarded as the dominant position in the chair behind the desk, his wary expression as he asked the question nevertheless suggested he felt the desk more of an entrenchment or a barricade put between them.

Mayo had no intention of being rushed. He settled himself comfortably and asked whether they had ever thought of expanding.

"No, not really. There's always a ready market for the traditional ware we make. We have as much as we can cope with. We're only a small firm, not like the big boys over in Stourbridge."

It sounded a fairly mechanical answer, and didn't square with what Bainbridge had hinted yesterday. Mayo said, "When I spoke to your office manager yesterday, I rather gathered you had some future plans, though."

"I'd like to do some reorganisation, yes, starting with the offices. As I told you the other day, we're short of space, and I want to computerise the accounts when Robert Bainbridge goes. He runs the place efficiently enough at the moment, but it's too much in his head. When he goes, we could be in dead trouble if we don't watch it. We need to reorganise the factory, too—not the manufacturing process, that's still basically the same as it always was—but the buildings are a shambles. They've been patched up for so long, there's nothing for it but start again . . ."

"What did Mrs. Dove think of all this?"

"She was coming round."

"That means she *hadn't* altogether agreed?"

"No, that's right—but my mother-in-law was inclined to put things off. She'd do anything sometimes rather than make her mind up, and you couldn't budge her. But I knew it was just a matter of patience."

"I see."

Dainty looked pointedly at his watch. Mayo said, "I've just one more question, sir."

"Yes?" The curt monosyllable couldn't hide the sudden tension that radiated from him, the wariness that sprang to his eyes.

"I've spoken with Mr. Crytch this morning and he tells me you've no objection to us knowing you were the principal beneficiary in Mrs. Dove's will."

"It won't be any secret anyway, when probate's been granted." Dainty smiled for the first time that morning. His shoulders almost visibly sagged. He'd been expecting a question, but not that. He obviously felt there was no danger in anyone knowing what the will contained.

It had in fact been brief and unsurprising. There had been several small bequests, and ten thousand pounds for Paul Fish on his eighteenth birthday, without conditions attached. Jubilee Cottage had been left to Mrs. Bainbridge, plus a generous annuity. Equal shares in the glassworks were left to her daughters, plus The Mount and the residue of her estate to be shared between them. But the majority holding in Dove's Glass was to go to Kenneth Dainty. Which might well be seen as a will heavily weighted in favour of the Daintys, as husband and wife. But perhaps Rachel had meant it, when she said she didn't care about money.

Mayo stood up. "We won't keep you any longer, sir. You've got to be at the inquest like me at eleven thirty, and you'll have things to do."

"Is that all you want?" Relief mingled with Dainty's evident surprise.

"Yes sir, that's all," said Mayo blandly. "Thank you for your time."

They left the building and Mayo waited impatiently for Kite, lingering behind, to join him in the car. "What kept you?" he asked as the sergeant eventually slid in beside him.

"It was that girl, Valerie. She's had something on her mind that she feels she ought to tell us. She nearly told you yesterday but she was too scared."

"Scared, of me?" Mayo wasn't sure whether or not he entirely welcomed the idea that he was less approachable than Kite.

"She feels as though she's being disloyal, telling tales, but anyway she told me that Mrs. Dainty came in on Friday, and she overheard some sort of quarrel between her and Dainty—more correctly, it appears it was Dainty who was doing the shouting, and he stopped when she went in, but she's sure they'd been arguing. Mrs. Dove looked upset and he was red in the face. And she quite distinctly heard the name of Steven mentioned."

The inquest went as expected. Dainty was called to give evidence of identification, medical evidence as to the cause of death was produced and the coroner, as was usual in such circumstances, adjourned the inquest for further police enquiries. The Press got a statement from Mayo which amounted to very little, but had to be satisfied with it.

Afterwards, he crossed the Cornmarket and went to the Red Lion where he had arranged to meet Kite for lunch, for no other reason than because it was usually less crowded than the Saracen's. He had barely seated himself before a hand touched his shoulder. Doctor Ison said, "I was told I should find you here."

"Henry, have you come to join us for lunch?"

"I don't eat lunch," Ison said virtuously, looking pointedly at the locally made faggots, mushy peas and chips which was the Red Lion's idea of gourmet food. Mayo ignored the look. As an occasional one-off, the meal wasn't going to put him in his box. In fact it was very tasty.

"You'll have a drink, though?" he asked. "What would you like?"

"I'd like a scotch but I'll have a non-alcoholic lager, please."

Ison in his most irritating mood, Mayo reflected. When Kite returned with the lager, remarking that he didn't know how the doctor could drink it, he said blandly, pointing his pipe stem at Kite's half of bitter, "You can get used to it, son. Better than that stuff you're drinking. Thickens your blood and gums up your arteries, that does. Stick to whisky, and your blood'll pour like the best claret through your veins. Cheers!"

"What can we do for you?" Mayo asked. "You don't usually honour us with your presence at lunch."

"No, but there's something about Marion Dove I think you might like to know, I remembered it just as I was getting into my car a few minutes ago. There's something been niggling me ever since she was found and then suddenly it came to me, just like that, you know how it does. It may not be of any significance, of course, being so long ago, but on the other hand . . ."

"Anything's welcome at this stage."

"That's what I thought." Ison fiddled with the pipe he had substituted for the cigarettes he had renounced on the premise that by the time it was lit the desire had gone.

"Get to the point, Henry."

"All right, all right, don't rush me, I've had a trying morning. The thing is, Marion Dove's been my patient a long time, but when I first joined the practice, that was in 1953, she was still under old Doctor Wade, the senior partner. When he retired, I took over his list, and that was when she became my patient. Before that, I only had occasion to see her once, when Doc Wade had 'flu and I was standing in for him." The pipe well alight, he leaned back. "She was expecting a child at the time and I was called out because she was haemorrhaging slightly, and there were obviously fears of a miscarriage. I did what I could, kept her in bed and so on and all was well as it turned out. I'd forgotten all about it until now."

"What's the connection?"

"The point is, it was her first child she was supposed to be having. I knew immediately that this was rubbish, of course, as any doctor would. But I also knew she hadn't been married long, and if that was how she wanted it to appear, and Doc Wade was going along with it, it wasn't my business to upset the apple-cart. One of the first things a doctor learns is to keep his mouth shut."

"When did she have this baby—the first, I mean?"

"It wasn't noted on her records. I assume that may be because she didn't have the child here, in Lavenstock. Was she away in the forces during the war?"

"Her sister was. I'll have it checked, but I had the impression Marion had stayed at home—she may have been on war work or something."

"It'll be the usual story, you'll see, father not able to marry her. A lot of that sort of thing had happened in the war—but that didn't make it any better for the poor girls, being an unmarried mother was a scandal folks would do anything to hush up, especially if they were strong chapel-goers, as I believe the Waldrons were. Mind you, it doesn't necessarily mean she *was* unmarried. For all I know, she may have been married before, but why then the secrecy? Anyway, that's your problem. I just thought you'd like to know."

"Yes, indeed. Thank you, Henry. It's very interesting." The doctor nodded, drank up and knocked out his pipe. Mayo put down his knife and fork and pushed his plate away. "Before you go." He hesitated, wondering whether to chance it with Ison, then decided he'd nothing to lose and reminded Ison what he'd said about Shirley Dainty being a neurotic woman. "Just how neurotic is she?"

"Hm." Ison looked at him consideringly for a while before answering. "Let's say I've been treating her for eight or nine years."

"For what?"

"Come on, Gil, you ought to know better than that! What I told you about Marion can't hurt her, she's dead. Breaching my living patients' confidence is another thing."

"It may be important, Henry. It won't go any further, you know that."

"It won't because I won't tell you. She has every right to demand privacy on this respect. Moreover, it's my considered opinion that her condition has nothing whatever to do with the enquiries you're pursuing," Ison said pompously.

And with that, Mayo had to be content. After Ison had left, he sat looking reflectively into his beer, thinking about what he'd just been told. "What would you do if you found you were terminally ill, Martin?"

"I'd want to see my kids and Sheila provided for, check up on her pension rights, make sure the insurance was up to date and so on," Kite said with unwonted sobriety. "Square my conscience, too, I suppose. If we're talking about Marion Dove, it's possible she might have felt she had to do the right thing by this illegitimate child, see him okay in her will . . . but my God, that would really put the cat among the pigeons, wouldn't it?"

"Very probably," said Mayo slowly. "In more ways than one."

Kite didn't have the imagination Mayo had, but he caught on quickly, and the possibility enlarged as he surveyed it. "We really have to find this Steven, don't we?—incidentally, I rang Dove's and there's no Steven on the payroll—though wouldn't he have more reason for wanting her alive, at least until she'd changed her will, rather than wanting to kill her?"

All the same, they had to find Steven, whoever he was, more especially after what Ison had told them, Mayo knew. He was perhaps making too much out of a name scribbled on the back of a till receipt, but he didn't really believe that. It could have been anybody's name, something totally dissociated with what had happened, someone coming to see her about decorating her bathroom, for instance, or something equally trivial. The note need not even have been referring to that particular Sunday, though there had been no date indicative of which future Sunday it might be. Much more likely in Mayo's mind was that the conjunction of events that combine to make what is called coincidence were all part of a pattern, one which had on that day led to murder. And that the mysterious Steven was an essential part of this pattern.

Chapter fifteen

Mayo banged loudly for the second time with Mrs. Bainbridge's shining brass doorknocker, then stepped back and gazed speculatively at the closed, gleaming sash windows before turning away and getting into his car. He was just about to click in his seat belt when the door of the next house opened and a young, mini-skirted woman emerged, pushing a pram on to the pavement towards him, waving him to stop.

"Hello, I heard you knocking next door. If you want Mrs. Bainbridge, she's gone back into work. Betty's, down Holden Hill Road, d'you know it?"

"Thanks—I do," Mayo told her, switching on the engine.

"You the police?"

"Now what makes you think that, love?"

"You must be joking! Well, if you do see her, tell her the telephone's been ringing half the day, somebody wants to get hold of her urgent by the sound of it. If she'd left me a key like she usually does, I could've answered it, couldn't I, but I expect she forgot, what with everything. Terrible about her sister, isn't it?"

These little houses, you could hear everything. Television, telephone. Babies crying. Family rows. He thanked the girl again, and drove off down the street and eased into the grinding traffic of Holden Hill Road. "Betty's" was a small shop with only one front window, not far from the confectioner's shop where he'd had tea with Rachel Dove, and he had to park round the corner in a side street. When he returned Mrs. Bainbridge was in the window, pinning a slim coyly posed model with a winsome face and outdated bouffant hairstyle into a dress of matronly proportions. The bell clanged as he pushed open the door, and when she looked up and saw him, she backed out immediately, careful not to disturb the other figures modestly draped in cotton sheets.

"Is it Paul, have you found him?"

He had to tell her they were still looking and watch her face settle into disappointment. But when he passed on the message about the ringing telephone, she brightened. "That'll be him," she said at once. "I knew he wouldn't just disappear, like that."

"Did he ever mention a girl to you, a girl called Katie Lazenby?"

"No, he never talked about girls, not to me."

"It looks as though they might have gone off together."

She looked first astonished, then relieved. "Well, that's more natural—more likely than running away because he killed Marion. I told you there was nothing wrong with Paul. Not that he's done right, mind, if that's what it is."

"There's still the question of your Visa card."

"Which he'll have to answer to me for when I see him . . . if he *has* taken it." She was still unwilling to believe that of him. "Give him time, he's sure to turn up."

Not necessarily, Mayo thought, but he didn't feel it incumbent upon himself to disillusion her by saying so. If Paul wanted to disappear, he could. If he were determined enough, strong enough. Afraid enough.

"I've something else I'd like to talk to you about, Mrs. Bainbridge, if you could spare me a few minutes."

"As long as you like," she said, turning the card on the door from Open to Closed, remarking that nobody else except her employer would expect customers today anyway, when everyone else around kept half day. She showed him into a small windowless room, part store-room, part kitchenette, at the back. Among a stack of cardboard boxes spilling tissue paper two little chairs, relegated to the back premises presumably on account of their chipped gold paint and rubbed silk seats, were squashed into the tiny space, together with a small flap table hinged to the wall, with an electric kettle on it, two mugs and a teapot under a cosy.

"There's some tea brewed."

Having declined the offer, and congratulating himself on his prudence when he saw the caustic nature of what she poured out for herself, Mayo gingerly lowered his large frame onto one of the fragile chairs before approaching his reason for being there. She sat opposite him, elbows on the table, the uncompromising fluorescent strip light overhead revealing lines on her face that grew visibly more taut as she listened to what he had to say. She heard him out, not interrupting. When he'd finished, however, she took him up with angry impatience.

"Haven't we enough to put up with just now, without you raking all that muck up?"

"Murder's a dirty business. Nobody can have any secrets, not even the dead."

Especially the dead.

"It's past and gone. It can't have anything to do with what happened to her."

He said patiently, "You must know that's not necessarily true. Your sister's been murdered and there's nothing about her life we can leave uninvestigated until we've found out why."

"What d'you expect me to say? You know all there is to know. She had a baby without being married. She wasn't the first and she won't be the last neither. Except nowadays they get rid and no disgrace if they don't want them."

"Listen, Mrs. Bainbridge. There was a baby, that much we know. What we need now is more detail—and you're the person who can most easily fill us out."

"And if I don't?"

"You'd be wiser to do so. I can't force you, of course, but we *can* find out from other sources, and they mightn't be so discreet."

She bit her lip. She was more upset than he'd imagined she would be. She knew about gossip and what it could do, and was dismayed, which surprised him, though perhaps it shouldn't have. Natural enough, he supposed, to want a family scandal hushed up, but who would really care, forty-odd years later? She was more concerned with her position in the community than he'd supposed.

He gave her time to think over what he'd said and in the end she gave in, albeit unwillingly, making him wonder at her sudden antagonism. When he'd questioned her before, she'd been upset, but cooperative, now she seemed actively hostile. "All right. It doesn't look as though I've much choice, does it? But I *don't* know much, and that's the truth. I was in the WAAF when all that happened."

"Let's start with what you do know. To begin with, can you remember the date the baby was born?"

After a moment's thought, she said it would have been early in 1944, probably about March. She had come home on leave herself in late April, and it was all over by then, Marion was back home.

It seemed that Ison had been correct in surmising the child hadn't been born here, and Mrs. Bainbridge confirmed this when he spoke the thought aloud. "Of course it wasn't! They'd concocted a story about her having some sort of nervous break-down—the after-effects of the bomb on Chapel Street it was supposed to be. They sent her away to our aunt near Wolverhampton to convalesce. Who did they think they were kidding, her not even home for my wedding? But it saved everybody's face. It would have killed our mum to have it out in the open, not to mention my dad. Little Marion, good as gold, quiet as a mouse—I reckon if it'd been me nobody would have been all that surprised, just because I liked a good time, though they'd have been wrong, for all that."

She pushed away her empty mug and scraped her chair back, swinging her legs round, preparing to get up. They were nice legs for her age, as he'd noticed before, and she was evidently not unaware of the fact. Her tights were sheer and her patent court shoes had high heels. "Well, that's about it, then. That's all you need to know."

"Not quite. What happened to the baby?"

"Adopted, of course. Abortions weren't ten a penny then!"

"Was it a boy or girl?"

"I have no idea," she said, looking at her watch, "and if that's all, I'd better get the shop opened again."

"Just a minute, I haven't quite finished yet. What about your aunt's name and address—"

"I don't even know if she's still alive! She must be a hundred if she is."

"All the same . . ."

Reluctantly, she told him. "It was Copley. Edith Copley. She wasn't really our aunt, only our mother's best friend. She was a district nurse, went to live near Wolverhampton when she got

married. I don't remember her address, but Marion used to
write to her at one time, I think."

"That'll be a start, thanks." The address book that had been
in the locked drawer in the bedroom might give them the answer. "Just one more thing, but the most important." He
paused. "Are you going to tell me who the father was?"

She eyed him sardonically. "Am I going to tell you what?
Well, maybe I would if I knew—but that's what we all wanted to
know, didn't we, and wild horses wouldn't drag it out of her.
She wouldn't let on, not even to me, though I could've helped
her. I *would* have, poor kid. That's all she was, a kid. Seventeen." She stared at the chipped varnish on her thumbnail for a
while, hesitated then said suddenly, "It was Wesley Dove, of
course."

"*Wesley Dove?* The man she later married?"

"It stands to reason. She'd started working at Dove's when
she left school. Maybe she was flattered he paid her attention, I
don't know. He was handsome enough in those days," she admitted grudgingly, "but he was married, though his wife was
sickly and he always had an eye for—for a pretty face," she
ended lamely.

"Don't you mean for a young girl?"

Her lips tightened. "How d'you get to know about that?"

"Oh, we hear things. But isn't it unlikely she'd want to marry
the man who'd given her such a hard time? Unless you mean
there'd been something between them all along?"

"No, I don't! Like I told you before, it's something I've never
been able to work out, why she married *him,* of all people, when
she'd plenty other chances—and turned them all down. All I do
know is she suddenly realized she wanted another child, she told
me she'd never be rid of the ghost of the other until she did.
That was the sort of thing she sometimes said, out of the blue, so
you didn't know how to answer. By then Wesley's wife was dead
and Marion had got to be his secretary, and what I think is she
saw her chances and reckoned she'd a right to something from
him, after all she'd been through."

It was possible, he supposed. Marion had been sixteen when
she found she was pregnant, the age Wesley apparently preferred a girl to be. And what Gwen Bainbridge saw as her rea-

sons for marrying him later was only confirmation of what Rachel Dove had told him.

"If he *was* the father then that," he said gently, "sounds suspiciously like a form of blackmail."

"Oh no! You'd have to have known Marion to understand. She wasn't vengeful. Never that. But subtle," she said, as if surprised that such a word had come to mind.

He put the next question in the expectation of getting a short answer, or none at all, and wasn't therefore surprised at her reaction. When he asked if either of Marion's daughters had known about this other child, her skin flushed a dull, dark red. "They do not—and I hope you won't go letting on! Especially to Shirley."

He could make no such promise. "We may have to," he had to insist. "But why especially not Mrs. Dainty? What's wrong with her?"

She looked very much as though she regretted her outburst, closing her lips with the stubbornness he was coming to see might well be a family trait. It had more than once been remarked so far during the investigation that Marion Dove had been stubborn, not to be moved, but he too was prepared to sit this one out. There had been too many dark hints about Shirley Dainty and her obviously neurotic condition. He waited, letting the silence lengthen, and finally unable to stand it any longer, she gave in.

"Oh, Shirley's all right. I get impatient with her, that's all. She had a bit of trouble a few years back, after little Michael was born, and I just think it's time she pulled herself together, but I wouldn't want to go upsetting her, for all that. She's had a lot to go through."

He kept his expression carefully non-committal, and with a sigh she poured herself another cup of tea and thus prepared, told him.

"Post-natal depression? Sergeant Thomson's wife had that, but it didn't last for ten years!" Atkins said.

"Nor did Mrs. Dainty's," Ison responded sharply. "Her case is somewhat different." He had called in at the station on a small matter of routine connected with the autopsy report and found himself involved, willy-nilly, in the discussion. He looked mightily as though he wished himself elsewhere. His face had deepened with disapproval when Mayo told him what he had learned from Gwen Bainbridge.

"We can take it as fact?" Mayo asked.

"Oh yes, it's true enough. She called me out one night in a terrible state. She was terrified of what she might do—what she might even have already done . . . she was in such a condition of collapse she couldn't even remember. I examined the child but I could find no evidence of any physical abuse. I believe she cried for help just in time . . . she had excellent treatment, she got over it."

Kite was doodling on the pad in front of him. "It can be hell, a baby who cries all the time," he said slowly, looking up. "Daniel was like that for a while, never seemed to stop, for no reason we could ever find out. They go on and on and there are times when you feel as though you'd do *anything* to stop them and get a good night's sleep."

"Only most people don't," Mayo said.

"Most people don't have the background she had," Ison retorted. "And anyway, she *didn't* harm the child. The nervous condition she suffers from is something quite different."

"We know about her background, we know her father was a violent man—maybe he used violence on her as a child." Ison didn't reply. "I don't want to push you further than you feel you've a right to go, Henry, but tell me this: Is she potentially dangerous?"

"I don't know what you mean by that. Things are rarely if ever so clear-cut."

"I'll make it clearer. Is her mental condition such that she would be capable of murder in certain circumstances?"

"Gil, I'm a GP, not a psychiatrist! Besides, that's a hypothetical question. You're really wanting my personal opinion as to whether she murdered her mother, and—very well, the answer's no. I believe the two incidents are entirely different and quite unrelated—but your own opinion would be just as valid. I'll ask you: Do you think she did?"

"I'm keeping my options open," Mayo said shortly. He wouldn't, whatever happened, let his compassion blind him.

Marion Dove's address book had been searched through in vain for the name Steven, as Christian or surname, but when Mayo looked through it this time, he met with instant success.

"Here we are, Martin, Mrs. Edith Copley!"

The address was an old people's home near Wolverhampton. A telephone call by Kite established that she was still there and an appointment made for him to see her the next day.

Chapter sixteen

Geoffrey Crytch's secretary was a Mrs. Lorne, of the breed which always seem to see their mission in life as being one which necessitates at all costs preventing anyone but themselves from having easy access to their employer. She informed Mayo with great pleasure that he'd just missed Mr. Crytch, who'd left for home five minutes before. He was lucky to have caught *her,* she was on the point of locking up, and no, she added firmly, she didn't think Mr. Crytch would be willing to see Chief Inspector Mayo at home. He'd had a very busy day. Why not make an appointment for tomorrow?

"Because I want to see him tonight!" Mayo had a short, sharp way of dealing with people like her, and Crytch wasn't the only one who'd been pressed that day. Over the indignant bridling that followed, he said, "Don't bother, Mrs. Lorne, I'll make my own arrangements with him."

Crytch had already arrived home when he telephoned and was about to have his dinner in half an hour, but agreed to see Mayo who promised he wouldn't keep him longer than that.

Kite, meanwhile, was on his way to the Dog and Fox. There were only a couple of cars as yet in the car-park when he arrived, neither registration less than ten years old. An elderly bull-terrier that might have been the progenitor of Charlie Fish's Caesar and a hundred others like him sat militantly by the door, a watchful, heavyweight Cerberus guarding the gates of Hades. Kite was allowed in and hoped he'd get out without losing a piece of his trousers.

The public bar looked as though it hadn't been redecorated since the Festival of Britain, the coco matting on the floor threatened to trip the unwary, the wallpaper pattern hadn't been visible for decades and the ceiling was pickled a rich brown from tobacco smoke. Two elderly men sat drinking Guinness beside a fireplace that contained nothing but a hopeless arrangement of tired plastic daffodils in a red glass vase. The landlord, Jim Littlebank, was at the bar in a washed-out navy sweatshirt that did nothing for his complexion or his figure. A silence fell as Kite entered. The police were known here and not liked, for manifold reasons. Kite ordered his half-pint (one of the reasons: they rarely drank more than halves), took it over to a corner table and opened his evening paper.

When he'd managed to down half his beer he folded the paper and went to the bar to begin his questions. "Police," he said, showing his card. The two customers began a game of dominoes.

"The fuzz, Rita," the landlord repeated to his wife. She laughed.

Kite gave her a look which suddenly made her busy herself with arranging the bottles behind the bar. She was Ruby Deacon's sister, and neither had much to crow about over the other.

The landlord's memory was short, his willingness to cooperate negligible, this being the second time the police had questioned him, the first time being in the course of their house-to-house enquiries. No, he disremembered Charlie Fish being in the pub any time on Sunday. On the other hand he might have been. He was so much a part of the furniture it was hard to say, especially when you were crowded. Very crowded they always were, weekends.

"What do they come for?" Kite asked. "It can't be the beer."

"What's wrong with the beer?"

"It's flat," he said, and went out.

Cerberus stood up and saw him suspiciously off the premises. It hadn't been the most successful interview he'd ever conducted, Kite reckoned, and the beer was sour on his stomach. He sat in the driving seat and stared round at the desolate landscape spread before him. Even in the golden hanging stillness of the furry-lit September evening it couldn't escape grimness. Even the knackered ponies in the field, cropping desultorily, seemed to have lost heart. He followed their progress, his eye coming to rest on the deserted brickworks three or four fields away, random and forlorn.

For a while, he let his thoughts wander, then suddenly some-

thing clicked and he jumped up as if scalded. That was it! He
grinned and buckled on his seat belt and put the key in the
ignition. A slight noise made him look round. Long red nails
like talons dipped in blood were scratching on the glass. The
publican's wife, Rita Littlebank, was peering in at the window,
her face distorted in an effort to gain his attention. He wound
the window down and her scent invaded the car, not cheap scent
either, but too much of it, musky and heavy.

"Here," she said, with a nervous glance over her shoulder,
"don't you go thinking Charlie Fish did that there murder,
'cause he never did. That's what you was on about, wasn't it?"

"And how would you know he didn't, missis?"

" 'Cause I know where he was on Sunday night, see." She
added unnecessarily, with a jerk of her head towards the pub,
"He don't like you lot, he wouldn't give you the time of day, but
he don't like Charlie Fish, neither, that's why he wouldn't say
one way nor another."

"Who's talking about Sunday night, just?"

"I am, aren't I? Because she was here on Sunday, about six,
and Charlie was—well, he was down my sister Ruby's then. I
know, I'd just left him there, and he stayed all night."

Kite said, "Let's get this straight. *Who* was here?"

"I mean *she* was here, Mrs. Dove, in the car-park, sitting in a
red Sierra. She was with a young feller, good-looking chap, he
went inside while she waited for him in the car."

Kite sat and looked at her, flashily dressed, her face raddled
with too much make-up, but good-natured enough. He didn't
think she was lying. "How well did you know her?"

"If you're thinking I could've been mistaken, I wasn't. I knew
her right enough, I used to work in the canteen up at Dove's,
one time. Nice lady, she was, and anyhow, we spoke to one
another. I said good evening and she asked me how I was. I
didn't stop, Jim'd already opened and I knew he'd be mad at me
for being late. The young feller came out with a bottle of gin in
his hands as I went in and they drove off."

"What time was this?"

"Just after six—about ten past."

"Why didn't you tell us this when we called round making
enquiries?"

"I wasn't here, was I? I'd gone shopping."

She could have let them know, all the same. But better late than never.

"Well, thanks, m'duck. Pop into the station and make it all official-like tomorrow, will you?"

"All right, but I don't want no thanks. Just, I don't want Charlie Fish blamed for somethink he didn't do. We used to be good mates once. He's a boozy old sod now, but you should've seen him when he was eighteen!"

Kite drove straight down to Milford Road and went immediately up to Mayo's office, but by that time Mayo had already left some time ago to see Geoffrey Crytch. After a moment's thought, he picked up the phone and had an interesting conversation with the person at the other end.

The Crytch home was a spacious and pleasant Edwardian villa in a quiet cul-de-sac within walking distance of the town centre. Mayo had left his car at the station, but was there within five minutes. There was no nameplate on the door, but he recalled that Laura Crytch was in partnership with several other doctors at the medical centre in the town. She answered his ring herself and showed him into a comfortably furnished room at the back of the house, where Crytch was seated at a grand piano playing Chopin and drinking sherry. The wide glazed doors stood open to a long garden with a manicured lawn and glowing, three dimensional flowerbeds throwing long shadows in the golden evening light, framed by conifers of artfully varied form and colour.

Mrs. Crytch was a tall woman, many years younger than her husband, with straight brown hair and a wide, lovely smile that beautified otherwise unremarkable features. She herself saw Mayo supplied with sherry and then after a few moments' conversation made excuses with commendable tact about seeing to the dinner and left him alone with her husband. Crytch's eyes followed her as she left the room.

"I won't keep you very long, sir."

The other man poured Mayo a sherry and apologised for stipulating only half an hour for the meeting. "It's Laura's day off, y'see, and we've a free evening for once. She's not on call and all the girls are away so I've none of this confounded ferrying here there and everywhere to do. Bought Jennifer, our second, a car for her birthday, but the others still have me on a bit of string." He smiled indulgently. There was a photograph of him, surrounded by a bevy of women, his wife and his four pretty daughters, on the table beside him. They could almost have been daughter and granddaughters. He added more soberly, "Have you found anything new—about Marion? I take it that's why you want to see me."

"We've come across something which may possibly have some connection, and yes, I think you might be able to help us."

"Oh?" Mayo felt that a distinct wariness had entered his tone.

"We've found out she had a child, long before she married Wesley Dove, whom we're trying to trace. We think she may have intended changing her will to include him. Is that likely in your view?"

Crytch's response was unexpected. His fair-skinned, already pink complexion became further suffused, and then the flush faded, leaving his skin mottled and unhealthy looking. He gulped down the rest of his drink. "I-I don't know whether that was so or not. She didn't say so to me."

"But you guessed it might be . . . an educated guess? Did you perhaps know about this child?"

"No, I—" Crytch picked up his glass, found it empty, looked round rather desperately for the decanter and poured another. Both his acquired lawyer's caution and his own natural savoir faire seemed to have deserted him. "Oh, God, yes. That is, there were rumours."

Mayo suddenly understood. "The child was yours."

"No! I don't know. It—it could have been."

Abruptly he jumped up and despite the warmth of the evening, closed the doors to the garden, shutting out the sweet, heavy evening scent of a white-flowered shrub near the door that Mayo couldn't identify, as if afraid his wife might suddenly have taken it into her head to eavesdrop outside. He was evidently terrified of her learning this secret he'd managed to conceal for more than forty years, a trivial one in today's world, but perhaps not to a man of Crytch's generation and temperament, who was also a lay preacher and a prominent member of the local Methodist church. To have it made known now would not only intrude into his tranquil, civilised and self-satisfied mode of living, it would reveal him as a humbug and a hypocrite, no longer the upright, respected citizen, or the ideal husband. It would do a lot of harm to his self-regard, Mayo could see, it would be a calamity.

Could such a humiliating prospect have stirred this mild man into violence? Unfortunately for Crytch, Mayo knew this to be entirely possible. He'd lost count of the murderers he'd met who looked as though they couldn't swat a fly. Moreover, he didn't allow himself to forget that Crytch was intelligent and shrewd, quite probably not as mild as he seemed, and was in a position to know more about Marion Dove's affairs than anyone else connected with the case.

"I'm afraid I shall have to ask you to tell me about it, please."

Crytch stared out of the window, at the picture book garden, saying nothing. "Very well," he said at last. His colour had returned to normal, but a dull, heavy, lassitude had replaced his usual smiling vigour. For the first time since Mayo had known him, he looked his age. "I'd been going out with Marion before I went into the army, as I told you, but you must realise I didn't know anything about any baby until I came out. It was actually my mother who told me. We all went to the same chapel, you see, Marion's family and mine, but my mother didn't like Marion—at least she thought she didn't come of a good enough family, but I was in love with her and I thought she was with me. All right, we were very young, but I swear it was genuine."

Footsteps approaching the door made him pause, but they went away again. "When I was called up she said she wouldn't hold me to any promises, we might both feel differently after the war had ended, but when I was demobbed and came home I still felt the same. I asked her to marry me, and she refused. I was pretty fed up about that, impossible to live with at home, I suppose, and that was when my mother told me what folks had been saying."

It all came out very smoothly, with practised courtroom fluency, but there was little doubt also that this was an oft-remembered tale. Remembered with resentment, the fires stoked up to keep the pot simmering? Mayo wouldn't have been surprised. "What about Marion herself? Didn't you ask her?"

"Not for a long time. Things had become different between us. She'd changed, there was no question of carrying on as we had before. She was unapproachable, she wouldn't let me touch her—we couldn't even talk. But one day I braced myself and asked her if it was true or not that she'd had a child, and if it were mine." He swizzled the remainder of his sherry round in the bottom of his glass, and then drained it in a gulp.

"What did she say?"

"She froze, then said she didn't want to talk about it, clammed up like an oyster and wouldn't say another word. After that we just saw less and less of each other until finally we stopped meeting at all. I could understand it in a way, her not wanting to have anything to do with me after what she'd had to face on her own . . . though she needn't have. If only she'd told me, it would have been all right, I'd have married her, she must have known that."

There was genuine regret . . . but underlying that, the shadow of an old, deep hurt. He had not, even yet, completely forgiven. It had taken him years to come to terms with his rejection, to reach the stage where he found it possible to marry. Would he have tolerated any possibility of disruption to his present happiness?

It all began to make sense, much more sense at any rate than believing Wesley Dove was the father. It explained Marion's refusal to marry Crytch, if she'd found herself pregnant and then discovered she didn't love him. That stacked with the sort of introverted, romantic young girl he'd come to envisage: a young girl strictly brought up and coming face to face with her own sexuality and its consequences. She'd be determined not to let her emotions run away with her ever again. That could be why she'd eventually married Wesley Dove, an arrangement of convenience, surely, committed solely to providing him with no more than a wife and the sons he hoped for to carry on his name, while she could have the children she longed for, the means of exorcising the ghost of her first child, as she had put it to her sister.

"Did she in fact tell you she was going to make provision for this child in her new will when she made the appointment to see you?" he asked Crytch. There'd be more to it than that, of course. More than a name in a will and a few thousand pounds as a sop to her conscience. Enough to make someone decide to stop her before she could make the change? And who was in a better position than Crytch to know about that?

"Not in so many words. She said, 'I'm going to right a few wrongs and tell you the truth. Poor Geoffrey, I ought to have trusted you before.' I've been in a panic ever since. If my wife and children got to know . . .'" Crytch pulled out a handkerchief and mopped his brow.

Mayo wished he had a fiver for every time he'd heard that fear expressed. Often a quite unjustified fear, if the wife—or the husband—was worth his salt. After all, what did this amount to? A boy and girl love affair, over forty years ago, with an outcome that wasn't so unusual. And if Mayo was any judge, Laura Crytch, who must have come across many similar happenings in her professional life, would not judge too harshly.

"I didn't kill her," Crytch said suddenly, desperately. Beads of sweat stood on his forehead.

Was he capable of it? On the face of it, he was woman-dominated, a role he apparently sought and preferred, perhaps patterned by his mother. When she had died, he had chosen another strong, capable woman in his wife Laura. His daughters also had him twisted round their little fingers. Even his secretary fell into the same category. But it would be a mistake to regard him as ineffectual. That he was not. He was a shrewd, clever and at the moment very worried man.

Mayo said, "I suppose you realize I'm going to have to ask you to account for your movements on Sunday, sir?"

Crytch looked out into the glowing evening garden, the white scented shrub sweeping to the lawn like a cascade of stars. "I was at home here all day with my wife. We did some gardening, I cut the lawn, trimmed the edges, that sort of thing."

"And in the evening?"

"We had dinner and read a little, listened to some music. Laura was called out for a while—it was an emergency. Some child who'd swallowed something toxic, I believe, and had to be rushed off to hospital."

"What time was that?"

"I think about eight—I don't remember, I dozed a little."

He went through it all again, questioning Crytch closely about the two hours between 11.30 and 1.30, but he had been with his wife the whole of that time. So Crytch, too, had had an alibi for the crucial hours.

He went back to the station to pick up his car and walked upstairs to see if anything had come in for him. He found Kite waiting in a state of excitement, and listened carefully to what his sergeant had to tell him. "You think she's telling the truth, this Mrs. Littlebank?" he asked.

"No reason for her not to, that I can see—and yes, I do think so. She's coming down to make a statement tomorrow."

So the murder must have taken place in the evening, which meant Crytch's alibi wasn't as watertight as he'd thought. Nor, for that matter, was Ken Dainty's. And what about Paul Fish? And the drunken figure Marty Witherspoon had seen? If Rita Littlebank's statement was to be believed, it couldn't have been Charlie Fish. But Charlie Fish, according to Kite, was in dead trouble anyway.

Chapter seventeen

Kite found the Aysgarth Home for the Elderly without difficulty, a big converted Georgian house about five miles out of
Wolverhampton town centre, fronted by a long garden and with
a large, sunny conservatory at the side where chairs were set out
and the old people were taking coffee. The matron, Mrs.
O'Shea, was a young and cheerful Irishwoman who took him
straight into her office, a comfortable chintzy room overlooking
the garden.

"I hope what I've got to say won't bother the old lady," Kite
said, after he'd told the matron briefly the reason for wanting to
see her, "I'll do my best not to upset her."

The matron laughed.

"Don't you worry about that, she's more than able to cope,
you'll find out. You'd like to be private, I expect, so I'll bring
her in here." She left him with a copy of *Good Housekeeping* and
returned a few minutes later accompanied by a neat little person, well below the level of Kite's shoulder, with carefully
permed white hair and small intelligent eyes like blackcurrants,
who was wearing a blue woollen dress with a pretty silk scarf
tucked into the neck. Kite found his hand gripped with surprising strength.

"You'll have had your coffee," she announced, seating herself
firmly in a high-backed chair, "so let's get on with it."

The matron said, "Now Edie, it's no trouble at all to get Mr.
Kite a cup."

"As a matter of fact I *have* just had one," Kite lied cravenly,
intimidated before he'd started.

"If you're sure, then? All right, I'll leave you to it."

Kite gathered his forces while Mrs. Copley summed him up
with her bright little eyes and then spoke to him.

"Well, let's hear what you've got to say for yourself, young man, I haven't all day. I've got me serial at eleven. What do you want to know?" She'd been away from Lavenstock for more than most people's lifespan, but it hadn't altogether robbed her speech of the local rhythms and intonations, and her voice was strong and without a quaver.

"All right Mrs. Copley, I'll be as quick as I can. Do you remember a girl called Marion Waldron, Marion Dove as she later was?"

Mrs. Copley gave him a withering look. "Of course I remember her. I might be ninety-one, but I'm not off me chump, not like some of 'em here. Got herself murdered, hasn't she? I saw it on the telly, and I said to meself when I heard you was coming, 'Edie, that's what that bobby's after.' It's about that baby she had, I suppose?"

"That's it," Kite said, leaning back. There were no flies on Mrs. Copley. He could see she had it all sussed out and he'd no objection to her making his job easier.

"Don't you go getting the idea she was a bad girl then, for a start. She wasn't, just unlucky that he couldn't marry her—or wouldn't. You lot, you men, you're all the same, you want your fun but you don't want to pay for it."

"Did she tell you who the father was?"

"She'd more sense! Wasn't much more than a kid herself, but she had her head screwed on the right way. I didn't ask and she didn't tell me. It was better that way. Anyway, she'd had enough of being badgered by the time she came to me. Her dad had shown her the back of his hand more than once, trying to get it out of her who was responsible, but she wouldn't let on. Never had much sense though, Bert Waldron, more concerned with what they thought of him up the chapel than how his daughter felt. Good job they'd me to turn to. Flo and me, that's Marion's mother, we'd always been good friends so it was natural she'd turn to me when she was in trouble, especially me being a district nurse and all. 'Sides, I was glad of the company, my husband and both boys being in the army."

Her bright eyes studied him. Suddenly she leaned forward. "You a Lavenstock man?"

"Born and bred there."

"Thought so, with that name! Any relation to Arthur Kite, worked up the waterworks?"

"He was my uncle, but he's dead now."

"I'd be surprised if he wasn't," she retorted, with the satisfaction of having outlived most of her contemporaries. "Cheeky young devil, he was. I expect you're the same, eh?"

"So they used to tell me," Kite replied, wondering how to get back to the subject, when she returned abruptly to it herself.

"Given half a chance she'd have kept that child, I'll tell you that, but you have to face facts and she knew it. It was a stigma, then, having a baby out of wedlock, she'd've spent the rest of her life living it down. I've seen enough of that in my time, and the trouble it brings. You made your bed and you had to lie on it in them days and it was best for everybody she let the baby go, but I've had children of me own and I know how she must've felt. Nearly broke her heart to let it go, it did."

"Where *did* the baby go?"

"That I can't tell you, 'cause I don't know. The vicar, the Reverend Archibald, he took care of all that. He knew somebody who was desperate for a baby and he fixed it up, all legal. It'd be a good home, mind, he wouldn't't've let the baby go to just anybody. Nice chap he was, he had ginger hair, looked like Mickey Rooney."

"Who?"

She leaned forward and slapped his hand. "I might as well've been talking to meself—haven't you been listening? The vicar of course!"

"I meant who's Mickey Rooney?"

She looked at him as though there was no hope for the younger generation, in particular those in the police force. "He was a film star, wasn't he? Used to sing and dance and that with Judy Garland. You've heard of Judy Garland, I suppose?"

"The baby, what happened to him?" Kite asked, holding on.

"Oh it wasn't a him." Mrs. Copley's indomitable old face softened. "It was a little girl she had, a beautiful little girl. Born into my own hands. She called her Rose." She fell silent for a while and then said suddenly, "You get used to the idea of death by the time you get to my age. It don't bother you so much. But strangled, eh? That's a terrible way to die. I was that upset when I heard. You hear about these things and you think well, likely they asked for it, but Marion wasn't that sort. She was a nice girl, and don't you listen to nobody that tells you different. Thoughtful, never forgot me, never failed to send me a Christmas card, she didn't—and this scarf last birthday. She had a bad start, poor wench—some folk seem to be born under an unlucky star and I used to think she was one of them, but it turned out all right in the end, didn't it? She married well, she had two more little girls. I was glad to know she was happy at last."

Kite saw no point in enlightening Mrs. Copley about the true state of Marion Dove's marriage. She seemed to have a low enough opinion of men already.

"Don't suppose you know where that vicar is now?" he asked without much hope.

"Oh yes, I can tell you that. He comes to see me now and again, though he's retired now. He's not as old as me, mind! He has a little cottage in a village called Shenningstone, know where that is?"

It was the other side of Lavenstock, but with luck, he might make it before lunch. He'd a hunch Mayo would want to go along, too.

"Is that all then?" Mrs. Copley asked, standing up in one brisk movement.

"That's about it." Kite rose too and thanked her for being so frank with him. "I'll get over to Shenningstone as soon as I can."

"I hope you catch him," she said, as he opened the door for her. Kite didn't ask who, this time. He knew she didn't mean the vicar.

A steady stream of elderly people met him in the corridor, making for an open door from whence issued the sound of a TV set advertising the newest, cleanest, whitest, improved, environmental-friendly washing liquid. It was 11.26. He'd timed that very nicely. Mrs. Copley would get to watch her serial after all.

The Reverend James Archibald was picking up windfalls in his garden, a back-breaking job for one of his age, and he was glad of the diversion when the telephone, connected to an outside bell, rang. After he'd answered it, he abandoned the apples altogether and allowed himself a few minutes' reflection, sitting on the wooden seat that encircled the apple tree, with the winey smell of the fruit all around him and the sun on his face.

It had all been so long ago, that impulsive act, the consequences of which continued to haunt him still. Marion Waldron. That young girl whose image wouldn't be dismissed whenever he had cause to examine his conscience. He wished Cecily were here, to reassure him that it wasn't his fault, that he'd acted in good faith and with the best of intentions. He might then be comforted for a while and believe the intention was what mattered. But Cecily had been dead these seven years, and now he had to wrestle with his conscience alone, or with God.

He was a simple man, a practical Christian who had always taken each day as it came and each person for what they were when they came under his pastoral care, and had left the probing of minds and motivations to others, and he only knew he'd been desperately sorry for the woman and her husband.

She'd been such an *intense* woman, Angela Feldon. She'd got into the habit of catching him at the church at every conceivable moment, she telephoned him at inconvenient times, she called at the vicarage and insisted on unburdening herself, she had declared that life meant nothing to her if she had no child to love, she needed fulfilment; it became an obsession and he'd feared that she really was in danger of taking her own life, as she threatened. How terrible it must be, he'd thought with compassion, to long for a child with such intensity, to know that it would always be denied. He and Cecily had been blessed with five children of their own, a source of love and delight that had withstood every trauma of adolescence and young adulthood.

So he'd done what he thought was best for everyone in the circumstances. It was only in the light of what happened later that he wondered guiltily if he hadn't acted as he did simply to get rid of her. Only very gradually and painfully did he later come to realize there were women, hysterical women, to whom anything unattainable immediately became a necessity they must possess, a terrible truth that he found very hard to accept: that it was possible for children, to some women, to be just another consumer product, that they had to have a child as they had to have a second freezer, or the latest food mixer.

A wasp, drunk on apple juice, buzzed round his ear. He wafted it away and after a while decided that self-pity was a greater indulgence than remorse and he'd better go and get himself cleaned up before the policemen arrived.

When Mayo pushed open the gate of the cottage just off the village street at Shenningstone just before lunch and walked up the path with Kite behind him, he saw an old man in a linen jacket sitting at a table on the small sunny terrace, a man spherical in shape, whose receding hair, eyebrows and eyelashes had all taken on that indeterminate dusty sand-colour between auburn and white. His pale blue eyes were a little rheumy, but his smile was kindly and benevolent, like a jolly old monk.

"Please sit down, Chief Inspector, Sergeant. You'll join me in a glass of sherry? It's a luxury I allow myself, a glass half an hour before luncheon, another before supper. Thereby I measure out my life like J. Alfred Prufrock." His smiling gaze travelled benignly from one to the other. "You don't know your Eliot? Ah well."

You'd imagine, Kite thought, that with all the time they have, these old folks, they'd be glad of something to fill it up. Measuring out his days! A poetry-spouting vicar's all we need. He felt relieved Mayo had thought it necessary to come along, watching the old man as he poured three careful glasses of the pale, dry liquid. He'd rather have had a glass of cold beer, himself, but he didn't like to ask.

"How can I help you?" He seemed a nice old boy. The tone was gentle, the voice cultured, an Eton and Oxford sort of voice.

Mayo said, "I believe I mentioned on the phone that it was about the girl you knew as Marion Waldron that I wanted to talk to you."

Archibald nodded, a crease of worry appearing between the sandy brows.

"Specifically, it's her child we're trying to trace."

"She hasn't been successful, then? I feared as much. She's making a mistake, after all these years, and so I told her."

"You told her? When was that?"

"Two or three weeks ago, maybe a month, when she came to see me. May I ask what your interest is in this?"

Mayo stared across the sunny terrace to the small orchard. The wind moved through the branches and lifted the leaves, and the apples still on the trees, almost at the peak of perfection, glowed like Chinese lanterns. "I don't believe you know what's happened, sir."

"Happened? What has happened?"

As gently as he could, Mayo told him. He could see it was a shock to the old man. He closed his eyes for a moment or two and Mayo wondered if he could be praying. Then he said, a little shakily. "That woman who was murdered was Marion Waldron? I read about it in the papers, but I never dreamed . . . You see, she didn't give me her married name. You know why I was the one, particularly, she came to see?"

"Presumably because you arranged the adoption."

The old man nodded, slowly. "She was adamant about finding her daughter. I thought she was making a mistake, as I told you. These things are possibly better left, after so many years, but she was very . . . well, she had her reasons." He didn't say what they were but Mayo guessed she had used her illness to persuade him into giving the information. Doubtless she could have found out herself, given time, but no-one knew better than she that this was something of which she had only a limited amount. "I see I shall have to tell you about it. It's not a pretty story, and I'm not particularly proud of the part I played in it, with hindsight, but I ask you to be patient while I tell you. May I give you another glass of sherry? No? Perhaps you'll take pot luck and have luncheon with me? Mrs. Wilson leaves me casseroles, always far too much . . ."

"Thank you kindly, but we really must get on," Mayo said. The old gentleman looked disappointed, but began his story.

And it didn't, after all, take long to hear how James Archibald, then rector of the parish where Edith Copley had lived, had helped to arrange for the legal adoption of Marion's child by a comfortably-off, childless couple who were desperate for a child of their own. How the husband had then been killed in the latter stages of the war, and the wife, a neurotic woman called Angela Feldon, left alone and with no-one to lean on, had been unable to cope. The child, the little girl Rose, had grown up self-willed and uncontrollable. The wilder she became as she grew up, the more her adoptive mother retreated and washed her hands of her. Finally, the girl ran away from home at sixteen to marry a disreputable young local tearaway called Steven Cordingley.

So 'Steven' now had a surname. "Where is he now—this Steven Cordingley?" Kite asked.

"He was killed, driving a car while he was drunk."

Mayo would have gnashed his teeth like Charlie Fish's bull-terrier, if it would have done any good. But there was *a* Steven, and maybe—"Do you know if there were children of the marriage, Mr. Archibald?"

"I believe there was at least one, a son."

"What happened to Rose?"

"I can't tell you that. I'd moved from the parish by then and it was only through reading about the crash in the papers that I knew of it at all."

"The Cordingleys . . . Steven's parents? Would they know? Were you able to tell Marion—Mrs. Dove—where she could get in touch with them?"

"I wasn't sure I could help her—that I ought . . ."

"But you did."

"Only as far as finding out where the Cordingley parents live now. I made some telephone calls while she was here, to people I still know in the parish. After that, I felt it was up to her."

"In the circumstances, sir, it would be helpful if you could pass on the address."

They left, ten minutes later, furnished with the address and each weighed down with a plastic carrier bag full of windfall apples which had been pressed on to them by Mr. Archibald, who wouldn't take no for an answer. Kite didn't want Mayo's share, and Mayo had no use for them, which meant, when they got back to the station, looking around for someone with a wife who'd be willing to make apple pies from his kindly meant but unwanted gift. To his mild surprise, it was Rhoda Piper who said she'd have them, in order to make apple chutney.

"It'll help start off my store cupboard when the house is ready. I'll let you have a jar when I've made it, sir."

Mystified, Mayo handed them over and she walked away before he could ask her what she meant. He asked Kite instead, as they walked upstairs. "She's getting married next month, they're buying one of those new houses by the river," Kite answered.

Mayo was astounded. Rhoda, getting married? She was all of forty, plain and worthy and somehow, if he'd thought of her private life at all, he would have imagined her as the sort of willing-horse daughter who'd been left by the rest of the family to take care of an elderly mother, the sort who'd never had the opportunity to get married, but who probably wouldn't want to, now.

"Her father's just died," Kite said, "been a semi-invalid for years, and now she's marrying this widower, not without a bit of money, either."

Mayo just stopped himself from grinning. "You do surprise me," he said.

It wasn't the only surprise of the afternoon. He'd been back in his office barely five minutes before the news came to him that Paul Fish and Katie Lazenby had turned up.

Chapter eighteen

He sat hunched on the hard, upright chair in the interview room with his head in his hands and wished he were dead.

He might as well be. His life was a total mess, he loathed himself nearly as much as he hated his father. He was useless at everything, he'd never be brainy like Gray, and what was worse, no way was he ever going to be able to pay for flying lessons. He couldn't seem to get one single thing right, not even with Katie Lazenby, and that was a laugh, when half the guys at school claimed they'd made it with her. (Though after the last few days he reckoned most of that was a load of bull.) And now his Aunt Marion was dead. Murdered. And the fuzz here were so thick they thought he'd done it.

He felt sick. It was like an oven in the room. They'd obviously just redecorated it and the hot sun on the windowframes brought out the pungent smell of new paint. And if Katie's father, the stupid old git, told him just once more that if he got his hands on him he'd have his guts for garters, he'd—he'd smash his face in! It was Katie's fault just as much as his, she'd been the one who'd needled him into taking Aunt Gwen's car in the first place, though nobody was ever going to believe that. The one who'd jeered when he'd lost his nerve and wouldn't use the credit card. He wondered what he'd ever seen in her.

She sat as if butter wouldn't melt in her mouth, next to her mother, who was wearing jeans and a T-shirt just like Katie, trying to look young, only she didn't. They were quite alike and Katie said they often passed for sisters. That was how Katie would look when she was old, it was weird.

He couldn't bear the thought of Aunt Marion being dead, he didn't want to think of it, because if he did he might blub, and they were already treating him like he was about twelve years old. He couldn't stop thinking about her, though. How they'd played chess, sometimes sitting for an hour without saying a word, that was brilliant. How he'd put up the fence round the duckpen for her and how she used to read poetry out to him. Not that he was into poetry—he hadn't understood most of it, but he'd liked the sound of her quiet voice . . .

He wished now he'd stayed away and never come back, let Katie come home on her own. Or that he'd agreed to do what Marion wanted and settle for that boring job at the glassworks. Maybe he might as well end up doing that, after all, if the offer was still open, it was what she'd wanted him to do . . . or he might even join the RAF, like old Mass had suggested. Probably he'd do neither, if he was going to make such a pig's ear of everything, he might just as well kill himself and be done with it.

"Let me just get my hands on him, the young devil!" Lazenby said again.

Paul didn't even raise his head.

"All right, all right, cut it out, Mr. Lazenby, please!"

Mayo had neither time nor inclination to listen while Rick Lazenby, the skin peeling off his nose from sitting too long in the unaccustomed sun, vented his feelings. He should have thought of that before he went off to the Algarve, and serve them right the holiday hadn't turned out as they hoped . . . the hotel hadn't come up to expectations, there was nothing to do all day except sit in the sun, the food wasn't up to much, either. Denise had caught a bug, she'd started worrying belatedly over leaving Katie, wondering if they'd done the right thing . . . and altogether, Mayo gathered, the holiday hadn't exactly cemented marital relations.

"We wouldn't have gone without her," the mother was saying now, defensively, "only the travel agents couldn't give me any other dates, and she had to be back at school, and we really *needed* this holiday, her dad and me. I've got a job in Catesby's office and I work hard—we both work hard—we like things nice at home, we're entitled to a nice lifestyle, we've done it all for her, anyway!" Denise Lazenby cast a look of venom at her daughter, who remained quite unaffected by it. "She's never gone short of a thing. I thought I could *trust* her!"

They were running predictably true to type, Denise Lazenby

and her husband. She was the dominant partner, while Lazenby just went along with her, both of them paying lip-service to his macho image. She'd be the one who paid the bills and decided on the holidays and had their social life planned to a T. Mayo was certain that her cool clever daughter, with her inscrutable eyes, was beyond her. She'd run rings round the pair of them, in fact. A right little madam, Atkins had said. Mayo, sitting opposite her in the interview room, wasn't prepared to argue.

She was a dark beauty, young Katie, with high cheekbones and vivid green eyes, slanting and thickly lashed. White-skinned and with her black hair bobbed and cut in a straight fringe, she looked like a pert, sexy maid in a French farce. Unlike Paul she was old for her age and self-confident, but underneath it still young enough to be very frightened at the moment, answering his questions meekly and with downcast eyes. Yes, Paul had rung her very late on Sunday night and begged her to go away with him first thing the next morning. She'd agreed in the end— just until her parents came home, she said, ignoring both her mother's indrawn breath and Paul's. He'd told her he could borrow his aunt's car, and said he'd plenty of money. She raised her eyes and Mayo saw a flash in them like the sun on a kingfisher's wings. "It wasn't true," she said, with soft scorn. "He hadn't any money, all we had was what I had with me and when that was gone we had to come home."

"What about that credit card of your aunt's, Paul?" Kite asked.

The boy made an attempt at evasion. "What credit card?"

"The one you pinched, right?"

"No, I never! I found it on the floor of the car and okay, that was what gave me the idea. But I put it in the dash and it's still there."

"That's true enough," Katie said, but the way she said it, it was as though she might have admired him more if he'd been prepared to forge the signature, to squander recklessly, to buy them the romantic, exciting time she'd envisaged when she'd agreed to go away with him. She was only fifteen, and for all her acquired sophistication, imagined that was what escapades like that ought to be. "We had to sleep in the car!"

Her father began, "By God—!" but Mayo interrupted him and spoke to the two youngsters.

"I'll be frank with you both. I don't much care what you've been doing this last week, as long as you've been within the law. You've caused us a lot of bother one way and another, but what I'm interested in now is what happened last Sunday."

"Nothing happened." The boy's tone was muffled. He was doing his best not to break down in front of the adults, and especially not in front of Katie.

Mayo decided to take pity on him, not for altogether altruistic reasons. He was certain to get more out of him alone, without all this flak from the opposition. He turned to Katie and her parents and told them they could go home.

"Is that all then?" Lazenby asked, the wind taken out of his sails. Yet he was relieved, both parents jumped up immediately, anxious to shake the dust of the police station off their feet as soon as possible. Katie seemed hardly to believe her good fortune, but to do her credit, she did appear slightly shamefaced at being freed and leaving Paul there. She refused to look in his direction, keeping her green eyes veiled.

"Inspector Atkins will do the necessary before you go—oh, and Mr. Lazenby, don't let's have any more threats against Paul here, eh?"

Rick Lazenby answered with a ferocious scowl at Paul that didn't impress Mayo. There'd be no more trouble from him. He'd got his daughter back, he'd gone through the necessary motions and wouldn't want any more bother. He must have known his own part in the affair wouldn't stand up to much scrutiny.

When Rhoda Piper had led them out, Mayo flung open the window and then resumed his seat. With more air circulating, and fewer people in it, the small room was cooler and reeked less of new paint. "Now," he began, turning to Paul, "let's have a talk about Sunday. Did you go down to the Jubilee to see Mrs. Dove at any time that day?"

"On Sunday? Yes. Well no, not properly."

"What do you mean, not properly, Paul? Make your mind up."

"Well, I went, but when I got there she'd got somebody with her, there was a car parked in the entrance to the lane, so I went away again." The lad seemed at last to be coming out of the stricken silence that had overtaken him ever since he'd walked into the room. He was a compactly built youth with a tanned skin and short-cut brown hair whose regular features hadn't yet hardened into those of the man he would become. He wore old jeans and a red T-shirt with "University of the World" printed on it. If Katie seemed older than her years, Paul was very young for seventeen. Immaturity still clung to him like the half-shed pupa case of a chrysalis moth.

"What time would that have been?"

"I don't know—round about seven I should think, but I don't remember for sure."

Mayo noticed he didn't wear a watch, so this was possibly true. "What was your reason for going to see Mrs. Dove?"

A spasm of misery crossed the boy's face. "I wanted to talk to her about something. I wanted her advice. She'd have understood, but I couldn't talk to her with somebody else already there, could I, so I went away."

"You'd had a row with your dad and you were upset, was that it?"

"Yes." Paul didn't ask how Mayo knew about it, he seemed to take it for granted that he would.

"Was it about money?"

"No!" The boy's fists inside the pockets of his tight jeans bunched with anger.

"It usually was, wasn't it?

"Well it wasn't this time! If you must know—it was something to do with Caesar."

"Your dog?"

"He's not mine! I wouldn't treat him like that if he was! It's sick, and I told him I was going to—" He stopped, flushing a dull red, aware that he'd gone beyond limits. "Oh never mind, I wouldn't expect you lot to understand."

"You were going to report him? Isn't that what you were going to say? Come on, what d'you take us for? We don't approve of dog-fighting either, lad. And not just because it's against the law."

Kite had been the one who'd spotted it, made the connection between the splendid dog, kept in fighting trim, with the sort of man Charlie Fish was, and put two and two together. Breeding fighting dogs for the ring was nothing new in this part of the world. It was a barbarous custom going back centuries, which

hadn't yet been entirely stamped out. It still cropped up sporadi-
cally, despite the risks and penalties. It had its appeal among
those who got their kicks from blood sports and illegal gam-
bling. Typical of Charlie Fish, this particular set up was haphazard, ill-organised and amateur, the abandoned brickworks serving as a venue, with the Dog and Fox being the only habitation
in the vicinity, where the landlord, whose suspected involvement with the dirty business of his customers had yet to be
proved, had almost certainly turned a blind eye.

Before the look of stunned surprise had faded from the boy's
face, Mayo said, "Don't worry about it, everything's been taken
care of, including Caesar, but things might not be very easy for a
while . . . I'm afraid your father's going to have to face
charges . . ."

"Tough," said Paul, but not with total conviction. Trying to
look as if he didn't care, he began to stand up, seeming uncertain as to whether anything else was required of him or not.

"Don't go yet, Paul, we haven't quite finished, but I'll not
keep you any longer than I have to. You'll want to be off home,
I expect."

The uncertainty was replaced by a sullen defiance as he
slumped back on to the chair. "I'm not going home, not back
there, I won't, not ever. My Aunt Gwen says I can stay with
them."

Mayo thought he might have expected that of Mrs. Bainbridge, but if Paul expected roses all the way, he was in for a
shock. There was trouble ahead there for him, too. But he
thought it would—in the end—be the best thing for all concerned in the circumstances.

Kite took up the questioning. "Let's get back to what we were
talking about. How did you get down to the Jubilee?"

"In the Mini. They let me use it, you know."

"Okay, I know. Presumably you recognised the car that was
parked in the lane on Sunday as belonging to someone who was
likely to be visiting Mrs. Dove? Not just anyone leaving it there
while they went for a walk on the canal bank, for instance—
otherwise you'd have gone down to the lockhouse?"

"Sure I recognised it. It was that silver D reg Peugeot of
Rachel's—Mrs. Dove's daughter."

There was no need to ask him whether he was certain. Any

boy of Paul's type and age could probably tell him not only the registration number and colour but also the condition of the tyres and the miles it had done, together with any optional extras it might have into the bargain.

"Was there any other car there?" he asked, thinking of the red Sierra in the Dog and Fox car-park in which Mrs. Dove had waited.

"Not unless it was right down by the lockhouse, I'd've noticed else. There's not much room for more than one at the top of the lane, and it's dodgy parking on the road, with the bridge and that bend there. But it's not a lane I'd take my car down, if I had one."

Perhaps it had been down by the lockhouse, all the same. Or perhaps Marion had simply been brought home, and the driver hadn't stayed. Perhaps he *had* stayed, long enough to murder her and leave her body behind him in the canal. Perhaps that was why he hadn't come forward. Perhaps . . . Mayo could think of at least half a dozen more variations of that little scenario.

There seemed little point in keeping Paul any longer. He was telling the truth. It didn't take too experienced detectives to realize that he was almost certainly innocent of any involvement in his aunt's death. They let him go.

"Where does that leave us?" Kite asked.

On one thing both men were agreed—the elusive Steven with whom Marion Dove had had an appointment had to be her daughter Rose's son, with the same name, Steven, as his father. And almost certainly, he was the man in the red Sierra. "He could easily have killed his grandmother after Rita Littlebank saw them in the car-park and got away before Paul arrived." Kite said.

"Then what about Rachel Dove?"

She'd lied about driving straight back to Northumbria, if only by implication, when she'd spoken to him. She had returned to the lockhouse that evening. He imagined her going into the house, finding it empty, searching around for her mother, as Percy Collis had done, and then finally discovering her. Easy enough to imagine. What he did find impossible to swallow was the idea of her simply leaving her mother's body, going back up north and carrying on with her normal life, packing for her holiday in Florence. Unless, of course, Marion Dove had still been alive when Rachel left her car and went down that steep path . . .

It was time to see her again. He was a fool to have allowed himself to pity her evident distress over her mother. That was when he ought, professionally speaking, to have pressed her more, but he had never been one to take advantage of another's grief, unless he absolutely had to. If it had been necessary, he would done it, but he hadn't deemed it so at the time and it was no use now wishing he had.

He decided on reflection however, his annoyance with himself having cooled somewhat, that it would wait a little longer. Kite deserved an evening with his family, for once. For himself, he was going to go home, cook a decent meal, listen to some music with a glass of scotch at his elbow and for the twentieth time go through the files, slowly and without interruption. He needed an overview, to see if, somewhere, he could find any connections or discrepancies in all the various reports and statements which had been made. He had this tantalising sense of pressure building up which told him they were very nearly there, but not quite. On the edge of discovering the key to the solution. Not by blinding intuition—experience had taught him this rarely, if ever, happened—but through methodically gathering the facts together and hopefully drawing a conclusion from them. He thought he might be in for a long evening.

Chapter nineteen

They were going to seek out Mrs. Cordingley this morning, at the address Mr. Archibald had given them. Mayo was up betimes, impatient to follow up the information Mr. Archibald had given them. It was a Saturday morning crisp and sweet and mellow as a September apple. A perfect day for the wedding Mayo wasn't going to. At least he'd remembered to make his apologies earlier in the week, and he'd found time to arrange for a greetings telegram to be sent to the happy pair. It wasn't very satisfactory, but it was the best he could do in the circumstances.

He'd asked Kite to meet him at Milford Road, but first he drove his car down to the canal-side flats and parked it there, having decided to walk through the tunnel towards the Jubilee Locks. He wanted to have another look at the murder scene, he didn't know that it could tell him anything, but he wanted to have another look all the same. It was necessary to test certain theories, to see whether they were as feasible as they'd seemed in the small hours, or whether they were merely the product of euphoria induced by a good malt and the glories of Elgar.

As he walked, he noticed *en passant* that yet another of the old factories had disappeared under the demolition hammer, revealing open spaces and an ancestral view of distant hills out beyond Henchard, hills once thickly forested, where deer had roamed and kings had hunted, but not for hundreds of years. Hills never before seen within living memory from this point because of the solid mass of tall brick factories, chimneys and warehouses that had obscured them. Soon they'd all be gone, these old relics of the Industrial Revolution, another new instant landscape would be created around the still raw-looking blocks of flats, bewildering the older generation, still accustomed here in Lavenstock to the slow imperceptible changes of time.

The new marina, where once a gasholder had stood, wasn't

waiting for this, it was already briskly in business. A few brightly painted narrowboats and several motor launches were moored in the basin, and outside the shop which catered for the boaters roses and castles bloomed on a new delivery of repro bargeware intended for the influx of visitors expected over the weekend. This was at present as far upstream as they could come, until the uncleared stretch beyond the tunnel and up to the Jubilee was tackled.

He came out of the darkness of the tunnel and into the bright morning and was struck by the notion of trying his hand sometime at painting the scene. He grinned to himself and the idea passed. He knew he'd never have the ability to depict the scene on canvas, to capture it as it was, tranquil and undisturbed as it might not be for long, the trees dappling the green water with sunlight, the old man fishing quietly on the bank. As he approached, Percy Collis caught a fish, removed it from the hook and threw it back. Perhaps it was too small, maybe the memory of what he'd found further down was still with him. They exchanged greetings and Mayo found a place beside him on the bank while the old man rebaited his hook and cast again into the water.

"Making much progress?" Collis asked when this had been accomplished.

"These things take time, Mr. Collis."

This attitude seemed to meet with Collis's approval. He was of that last age to whom it seemed right and natural to take your time over everything. They sat in companionable silence for a while. The old man remarked, "Days like this, I can see why her wanted to live here. Not much of a place, but better'n rattling round in that bloomin' old mansion next the glassworks."

"Or Chapel Street, so I've heard. Folks I've talked to seem to think that bomb on it was a blessing in disguise."

"It wor that orright—though we didn't think so at the time."

"You'd never forget a night like that," Mayo agreed.

"Suppose not. Surprising though, how much yo' do forget, good thing too, I reckon." What he was saying, of course, was that memory had of necessity to be selective. No one person could bear the weight of every single remembered misery, such as were witnessed in wartime. Mayo could wish his own memory was, at that point, slightly less selective, he could do with remembering everything that had been said to him during the last week.

The old man suddenly gave a reminiscent chuckle. "Funny thing, what I've never forgot about that night is how it spoilt my Whit Sunday dinner! My missis'd been lucky and she'd got a chicken for us, see—a real luxury in the war. Being in the ARP, I'd spent all Saturday night getting injured folks out and somehow it didn't seem right, tucking into chicken and that next day, Whitsun or no."

There was a tug on his line. For several minutes he was occupied with more immediate matters. Again the fish was landed, then thrown back into the khaki coloured water, the hook rebaited, the line cast. "And that soldier. I do remember him. And I can still see Marion, only a bit of a kid as she wor then, but more guts than some o' the lads, that night."

"What soldier was that, then?"

"Dunno who he could've been, never saw him after that, not that I know to. We was all black as the ace o' spades with all the smoke, yo' wouldn't've knowed your own brother that night. But a real hero he turned out to be. Funny what yo' remember, ain't it?"

Mayo left old man Collis and walked along the overgrown towpath to the lockhouse. He walked around, he looked at the crumbled bank and the slimy lock gates, he assessed the steep, stony lane and the slippery stairs by the side of the lock. And as he stood by the green painted fence and looked up at the red rocks and the loose, unpromising shaly soil from which the tall, graceful trees had sprung and flourished until they now formed a deep and bosky green glade, he wondered, with a sense of loss, what would happen to the lockhouse now. Gwen Bainbridge would try to sell it to help finance her bungalow . . . if they could find anyone prepared to live in such a place, knowing a murder had been committed here. But of course someone would be found, despite that, despite the desolation that now seemed, even on a morning like this, to hang over the cutting, perhaps people who'd turn it into another weekend cottage, whitewash the outside and prettify the inside, build a garage where the kitchen garden and the duckpen had been and lay down a proper drive from the road. He noticed the ducks had gone, and wondered whether Kite had got someone to take care of them, or if a fox had had them. He must remember to ask. It seemed important to him to know that her ducks would be looked after.

Kite was ready for him at the station, but Mayo asked him to wait and went upstairs to his office. He wanted to make arrangements to see Rachel Dove immediately when he got back. But first, what had she said on her official statement?

Nothing, he found when he looked for it, because the statement wasn't there.

"She was supposed to have come in yesterday to make it," he told Atkins.

It appeared that she had not. Further enquiries elicited the fact that not only had she not been in to the Milford Road station, but that she had in fact left Lavenstock.

She'd been asked to come in and make her official statement, she'd been asked not to leave Lavenstock without informing the police. She'd done neither. Nor did her sister know where she had gone, when Mayo, tight-lipped, had Kite make a detour round by Henchard because he wanted to speak to Mrs. Dainty himself.

Ken Dainty wasn't at home, and a cleaning woman was busy in the sitting room, so she took them into the kitchen, a miracle of modern technology allied to olde worlde nostalgia. They were offered chairs that matched the stripped pine table in an alcove papered with Victorian rosebuds while the washing machine and the dishwasher clicked and sloshed through their various programmes, and the fridge and the king-size freezer hummed in concert.

"You've no idea where she's gone?"

"No," she said, pouring coffee from a fancy glass jug with a plunger device.

"Has she gone for good? I mean, is she coming back tonight?"

"How should I know?" she answered tightly. "I'm not her keeper!"

So they'd quarrelled. About the will? Had death, instead of bringing them closer, caused a rift, as it so often unhappily did?

She was getting worked up. She'd drunk her coffee, hot, black and strong, before Mayo had started his, and nearly smoked through a cigarette. After what he'd learned yesterday, he was disposed to try and be more gentle with her than her attitude to him warranted, but he was decidedly fed up with chasing after the various members of this family. "Didn't your sister leave an address?"

She was twisting a dull, inexpensive-looking little gold signet ring round and round on her finger. She saw him looking. "My mother's," she said, and her eyes filled with tears. It was at this point, Mayo realized later, that he'd begun to feel sorry for Shirley Dainty. Up to then, she had merely irritated him, and there was really no reason for him to feel otherwise now, but he did.

No, she'd left no address, but there was someone, Mrs. Dainty said, either relenting or sensing the change in his attitude, who might just know where she was. His name was Josh Amory, Dr. Amory, and Mayo could get him at this number at Northumbria.

Josh Amory. He knew the name, he'd seen the man presenting a very enjoyable television series of programmes on Renaissance art. He rang the number he'd been given from the car, expecting to hear the pleasant voice with the amused, ironic note he remembered. He let it ring twenty times, but there was no reply.

It was clear from the start that Mrs. Alma Cordingley was not one of the world's fighters. She had lost the battle with the hem of her skirt, her wispy grey hair and her ill-fitting false teeth, through which she spoke with almost closed lips, as if afraid they might otherwise snap out and savage her unawares. Her thin figure drooped hopelessly, her face was anxious. In the struggle for respectability however, hers was the victory. Alone in a neighbourhood not renowned for its salubriousness, her house shone with conspicuous cleanliness, the tiles in the tiny porch were a gleaming cardinal red, the white lace curtains stiffly crisp and spotless. A washing machine whirred in the background as she let them in. A Hoover stood at the foot of the stairs.

She perched on the edge of a straight chair in the evidently little-used front room, where the three-piece suite was protected with antimacassars embroidered with lazy daisies and the only picture in the room, a print of a malevolent-looking Persian cat, hung two feet above eye level. Yes, she confirmed, Steven Cordingley was her grandson. Yes, he was over here from Canada. No, no, not *staying* with her, she couldn't do with him here! she exclaimed in fright, as if looking after her grown-up grandson would be a task as totally beyond the scope of her abilities as sailing single-handed round the world. It probably was, poor woman, Mayo thought; thirty years younger than she was now, she hadn't seemingly had much success in handling her son.

"Presumably you know where he's staying?"

"He's taken a furnished flat somewhere over the other side of the town. I have the address if you want it, and the telephone number."

"Thank you, Mrs. Cordingley, that would be most helpful."

She gave them the details, taken from a postcard kept in her handbag. "He—he hasn't got himself into trouble, has he?"

"Not that we know of."

"Only—I hope I've done right. When that woman came—the one said she was Rose's mother—I didn't know what to do. I had to tell her Rose—my son's wife—was dead, see, and I could see it upset her, but she still wanted to know all I could tell her." She hesitated, fiddling with a button on her cardigan. "You know Rose was adopted as a baby?"

"Yes." So Rose, too, was dead. Somehow, Mayo had half-expected it.

"She was upset about that, but so was I, when she died, you know." Momentary rebellion lifted Mrs. Cordingley's defeated shoulders. "She'd never known Rose, but I'd grown fond of her, in spite of everything." Her mode of expression was limited, she wasn't given to extravagant phrases, but Mayo knew immediately that she had loved the girl and resented the real mother who had, as she saw it, deserted her baby. "She'd made such a big effort to put herself to rights after Steven was killed. It was that car crash did it, made her realize what sort of life they'd both been leading, though the crash was his fault, he was drunk when it happened. He was always wild, Steven, I always knew he'd come to a bad end one way or another." Her lips tightened against emotion. "But Rose knew she had to pull herself together for the sake of the child, and when she said she was

going to try to make a new start in Canada, I encouraged her. I
didn't want to lose them, but it was best that way."

She shivered and pulled the cardigan closer round her thin
shoulders. It had evidently been a long speech for Mrs. Cordingley. She looked exhausted. Mayo said gently, "What happened
to her over there?"

"Oh, she knocked around a bit. I don't think everything came
all right straight away, but she got married again after a while,
chap called Jack McKinley. Well she would, she was a lovely girl
you know, always laughing, full of joy. This is her and Steven,
and the baby, taken on her birthday. 'I only have a birthday
once every four years,' she said, 'so I'm going to have a real
celebration.' A leap year baby she was, see."

Mayo looked at the photograph she took from the place of
honour in the centre of the sideboard. Even by flash, you could
see that Rose was smiling and dark and vividly beautiful, and
not in the least like Marion Dove's other daughters.

"See what I mean?" Mrs. Cordingley, who could never have
been beautiful, and couldn't have had much joy in her life, gave
the photograph a rub with the corner of her apron and put it
tenderly back.

"So what happened after she married McKinley?"

"She seemed very happy, and after a bit she wrote to tell me
she was having a baby. She died having it, and the baby as well,
you don't hear of that so much nowadays, do you? Maybe she
was a bit too old, she was getting on for forty. They said there
were complications."

"And young Steven, what happened to him?"

"Well, he didn't keep in touch with me like his mother had
but then he'd never known me, really. He was only a baby when
they left. I was just a name to him. He stayed with his stepfather
for a while after his mother died, but I don't think it worked
out. He seems to have done all sorts of things since. I gave
Rose's mother Jack McKinley's address and that's how she got in
touch. Steven called to see me when he came over from Canada
about six or seven weeks ago." She didn't sound as though she
expected him to call again.

Mayo stood up. "Thank you Mrs. Cordingley, I don't think
we shall need to trouble you any more."

Relief was evident as she smiled her closed-lip smile and

showed them to the door. However curious she was, she hadn't asked them why they wanted to know about Rose, nor even much about Steven. She'd had her troubles and wanted no more. She closed the door firmly behind them and the Hoover started up before they reached the gate.

"There's another one who didn't seem to know about the murder," remarked Kite when they were in the car.

"There's no reason why she should have made the connection, any more than Mr. Archibald did, if she didn't give her name. I saw no need to tell her, not at the moment at any rate, no point in it."

Mayo spoke absently. He agreed with Kite that Steven Cordingley would have to be picked up and brought into the station, and then fell silent, staring unseeingly through the windscreen as the car sped towards Lavenstock. After a while, he asked Kite to get someone to find out details of Geoffrey Crytch's army war service and his leaves. "It's possible he could be this soldier that Collis remembers."

"Crytch?" Kite whistled softly. "I'll put Farrar on to it, it's just the sort of job he enjoys—but he won't be able to get much over the weekend." He made a swift calculation. "That would be May, 1943, I take it? Nine months before February 29th, 1944?"

"Whitsuntide." Mayo tried the call to Northumbria once more. There was still no reply. After which, Mayo relapsed back into a deep silence, breaking it only to ask, "What happened to those ducks?"

"Which ducks? Oh, they've gone to a farmer the other side of Brome who has a flock. By the way, he says they can't exist long without water. They ought to have it for swimming in, but it's not essential. They must have plenty drinking water, though, and deep enough to immerse their heads when they drink."

"Interesting." But it didn't really matter now. The limits within which Marion Dove had died had been established as no more than thirty-six hours, but Mayo thought he could pinpoint the time now more exactly than that. He was almost certain now he knew when she'd been killed, and why and who the killer was.

Another call to Northumbria when they got back produced the same negative results. Mayo decided to give it another day —Amory might be away for the weekend—and then enlist the help of a friend and colleague who lived in the area.

Chapter twenty

So here he was at last, Steven.

Steven Cordingley, twenty-six years old, tall and narrowly built, with dark straight hair, good teeth and the sort of mid-Atlantic accent that said he was not anxious to be classified as belonging to one side or the other. A young man whose life had been such that he found it hard to settle anywhere, who made no allegiances as a matter of principle, perhaps never would. He smiled often, but fleetingly, and never with warmth. His eyes considered, explored, rejected. He held a kind of violence contained within his thin, taut body.

He refused tea or coffee and sat silently opposite Mayo in his upstairs office, chosen because the decorators hadn't yet reached here, and there was no paint smell. Two of the DCs, Pete Deeley and Nick Spalding, had been sent out this morning to fetch Cordingley and they'd only just returned. He had, he explained, been busy trying to book himself a seat back to Toronto.

"Not even staying for your grandmother's funeral?" Mayo asked.

He shrugged. "I don't go for that kind of thing." He had the kind of eyes, though his were very blue, that reminded Mayo of Katie Lazenby's. He found it very hard to trust anyone with eyes like that.

It was less odoriferous than downstairs, but the room was still very hot. The air conditioning seemed to be having another of its go-slow periods. Kite opened a window experimentally, but closed it immediately. It was marginally better without the traffic noise from Milford Road.

"Well, Mr. Cordingley, I'm waiting."

"I don't know what you want to know, for God's sake."

"Don't play games with me, I've other things to do with my time. I've told you once and I'll tell you again—I want to know

exactly what happened from the time your grandmother first
contacted you, right up until last Sunday, the day she was killed.
Exactly one week ago today, when you were the last person
known to have seen her."

"I take it this means you think I killed her, but you'd be
wrong. I wouldn't do that, I liked her, I really liked her. We'd
got to be friends . . . it didn't seem like she was my grandmother at all—"

"Mr. Cordingley, *if* you please." Mayo took all this with a
pinch of salt. "Stick to the facts for now."

"If it makes you any happier." Cordingley stuck his hands in
his pockets and leaned back, digging his heels into the carpet.
"She wrote me about eight weeks ago and told me who she was.
She asked me to come over as soon as I could and sent me the
money for my fare. I was knocked over . . . I'd no idea there
was anything like that in the family background and I was intrigued. I'd always intended to trace my family if ever I got the
opportunity, find out what kind of genes I'd inherited. It's important to know what kind of genes you have, don't you think?
Well, I came over immediately, there wasn't anything particular
to keep me in Canada."

"Isn't that a long time to take leave from your job? Two
months?"

"Luckily, I'd quit the job I was in a couple of weeks before I
heard from her." He offered no further explanation for what
seemed a fortuitous occurrence. A timely leavetaking, Mayo suspected, capable of varied interpretation as to the exact date.
He'd be willing to bet Cordingley had packed his job in as soon
as he heard from Marion, he wouldn't have been able to wait to
see what was in it for him. It was unlikely that Mrs. Dove would
have told him what her intentions were before seeing him.

"Carry on, please."

"I contacted her as soon as I arrived over here, we struck up a
rapport, and that's all there is to it."

"A little more than that, I fancy."

"What's that supposed to mean?"

"I believe Mrs. Dove has been very generous to you, finan-
cially, over the last few weeks."

"She helped me out a little, yes. I had to have somewhere to
live—"

"And a car?"

"It's on hire."

"Still costs money. But I think there was more, wasn't there, Mr. Cordingley? I think she indicated that she was prepared to provide for you in her will and that's why you hung around."

The young man threw him a narrow look, leaned back and folded his arms. He wasn't smiling any more. "You think so?" he said. "Then you're way out. I wasn't interested in any long-term projects."

"Perhaps you'll be good enough to tell me what you were interested in."

"Why not? She offered me a stake in the company—a marvellous chance, something right up my street, that would really give me scope. I could hardly believe it! She took me round the works a couple of times, but it only needed once to see the potential. They're dead from the neck upwards there, you know? So laid back they're damn nearly asleep. There's Ken Dainty, a wonderful craftsman but steeped in that damned family tradition, no ideas about branching out. Why do they need to keep to crystal ware, when the world's crying out for industrial glass, for instance? Money, he says, that needs money, to launch into something like that. My God, go in with one of the big conglomerates and their troubles are over! But he would never agree to that, he's still got the last five hundred years round his neck. And that old guy Bainbridge in charge of the offices! I tell you, they haven't seen anything like him in Canada in a hundred years. What it needs at Dove's is a clean sweep, something to take them into the twenty-first century, and forget the last five hundred years, for once. And she was going to give me the chance to do it!" His face had set with fury. "So why, may I ask, should you think I killed her? I'd every reason for keeping her *alive!* What do I get now? Damn all."

"What did Mrs. Dove say to these ideas of yours?"

"We didn't discuss that side of things."

No, they wouldn't have done. He would have been careful not to. He knew just which side his bread was buttered on, this young man, and he wanted the jam as well. He'd have been careful to have his foot in the door before doing anything that might prevent his getting it.

"Tell me what happened on Sunday. Exactly."

Cordingley had swiftly regained control. His white teeth
flashed in one of those smiles of his as he said, "I'd told her how
I liked Lavenstock, that I was growing fond of it, and she said it
was high time I saw some of the real English countryside, so we
arranged to go out for a drive, at about two o'clock."

"Two? Not earlier?"

"No, it was two, though originally we'd arranged to start out
mid-morning. She usually went to her sister's for Sunday lunch,
but she'd cancelled that."

"Is that what she told you? That she'd cancelled it?"

"That's right."

This was a point that had troubled Mayo from the first. Marion Dove hadn't seemed to be the sort of person who would
simply not turn up for a lunch when she was expected without
apology. At first it had been assumed this was because she was
dead by then, but now they knew she was alive until six at the
least. And if Cordingley—who appeared to have no reason to lie
about it—was correct, then why had Gwen Bainbridge kept the
meal waiting? Or *said* she had?

"But she rang me and said someone—her daughter, to be
exact—was driving down to see her from that place Northumbria where she teaches, and would I mind if we started out later,
in the afternoon. It was a little early when I got there, about
one-thirty. I fed the ducks for her while she changed, and then
we went out."

"Where did you go for your drive?"

"Oh, we just drove around through the country lanes, had a
pot of tea and a toasted teacake at a little place in the Cotswolds,
and then came back. It was a lovely day and we didn't hurry. We
got back later than we intended."

"When, exactly?"

"I don't know, exactly. Just after six, I guess."

"Where did you park your car?"

"Right down by the house. Not where I normally left it, but I
had to leave room at the top for the others."

"Others? What others?"

"Oh my, haven't they told you? Ken Dainty—and Marion's
daughters. I'd met Ken a couple of times at the works, as I told
you, but not the daughters. They were all supposed to be down
at the lockhouse for seven-fifteen, so there could be a grand

introduction. She was going to tell them formally what she intended to do."

"I see. Did you call anywhere on your way back?"

"No. Apart from that ratty old place up the road, the Dog and Fox, to pick up some gin. I'd noticed before we left she only had a couple of shots left in the bottle and Ken's capacity alone is more than that. I'd an idea I was going to need more than that myself. It didn't seem to me the meeting was apt to go very smoothly."

"You mean because Mr. Dainty was likely to oppose your introduction into the firm?"

"Well, I knew that already! But I suspected there was something else. Marion hadn't been herself all day. She seemed moody and she'd been probing into my past, wanting to know why I'd had so many jobs and all that. I told her, nobody stays with the same firm half a century like old Bainbridge nowadays. And of course, it all came out when the others arrived. Dainty, the slimy bastard, had had enquiries made about what he called my track record. Well, you can cook up anything to look bad if you want to! The upshot of it was that Marion couldn't bring herself to tell them what she'd promised me she would. I tried all ways to get her to say but she refused to discuss it. In the end I lost my temper a little."

His frankness, maybe because of the way he projected himself, was suspect, posing the question of why he should want to lie. Again he smiled. "I could see *that* wasn't going to do my prospects any good, so I decided I'd better leave and go and think it all over. Dainty said not to bother, they were going anyway, he and Shirley had this dinner party and were already late. Rachel went too, she'd driven them all down to her mother's and she had to get back up north."

"So you were left alone with Mrs. Dove?"

"I was, but I'd calmed down by then. I tried to get her to see reason, but she wouldn't promise me anything. She said she needed time to think, and in the end I had to be content with that. I helped her to clear up before I went. I was just getting into the car when she came running after me, waving her bag. She had five hundred pounds in it that she'd promised me and forgotten to hand over. I almost told her to take it back, but I didn't want to start anything up again, and there was the rent for my apartment, Lord knows what else . . ."

He'd known how to get round her. Feeding the ducks. Helping to clear up. And had been well rewarded. "And that's all that happened? Are you sure your quarrel with your grandmother didn't escalate and end with your strangling her?"

Mayo waited for the outburst, which surprisingly wasn't immediate. But it would come, soon enough. Cordingley was fluent and plausible, he wouldn't waste time that he could otherwise use to justify himself. But he took his time, and when he did speak, his natural arrogance seemed to have drained away. "I just can't believe this! Two months ago I was in Toronto, not exactly living it up, but at least I was free. And now I'm in this mess, suspected of murder!"

"If you're innocent, you've nothing to worry about," Mayo assured him, a statement he'd always considered particularly inane, but which, in the circumstances, he considered was fair enough.

"You really believe that, do you? I've heard of British justice. I guess I'm not seeing much evidence of it. No, I didn't kill her! I did not!" Sweat stood on his forehead.

Mayo asked suddenly, "You seem to have become very close to your grandmother . . . did she ever tell you who your grandfather was?"

It was the sort of random question that was apt to rattle witnesses and for a moment Cordingley seemed disorientated by it. "No," he answered, recovering quickly. "I wasn't interested."

Mayo had to listen to a lot of lies in his job. He would have imagined Cordingley would have made a better shot at this one, would have remembered sooner that he'd just said it was something he'd always intended to do as soon as he got the chance. He was remembering it now, too late.

Mayo had heard enough. This was as far as he was prepared to go at this point. "All right, Mr. Cordingley. Sergeant Kite here will get your statement typed and when you've signed it you can go."

"Go?"

"What d'you expect, bed and breakfast as well as a ride back? But if I were you, I'd cancel that ticket back to Canada. You're not about to cross the Atlantic yet a while."

When Kite returned from following out his instructions an hour later, he found a message from Mayo who had, for some reason best known to himself, decided to have another look at The Mount on his way home.

He had opened his desk drawer and found the big, old-fashioned key to the house staring up at him. It had been there since his first visit, waiting to be returned, and he must have opened the drawer dozens of times since without actually being aware of it, but now he picked it up, weighed it on his palm for a minute, then pocketed it and went down the stairs to his car.

He didn't need the key, after all. There was a car parked in the drive, a big, ten-year-old Vauxhall with a Leeds number-plate, and the front door of the house stood wide open. Some of the windows were open, too, letting in the evening sun that was shedding a misted radiance over the garden. The acrid smell of a bonfire was strong on the air. Smoke blew over the gate that led to the back of the house. He raised his hand to bang the knocker, but before he could do so, a man in shirt sleeves and corduroys came out through the gate.

This was no jobbing gardener. Mayo knew him at once, though he was taller and much thinner and altogether more ordinary than he'd appeared on the television screen. That phone call to his colleague wouldn't be necessary now. "Dr. Amory?" Mayo introduced himself and the man smiled and apologized for not shaking hands, spreading his own, begrimed from the bonfire, in explanation.

"I suppose you want to see Miss Dove?"

"If she's here, yes, I do. I've needed to see her for the last couple of days."

Mayo felt himself being assessed with a sharpness that wasn't disguised by a pair of horn-rimmed spectacles and a mild manner. You could wilt under a scrutiny like that, if you were maybe a young student, unsure of yourself and how your opinions were being received, but Mayo was made of sterner stuff and said, "And I'd rather not waste any more time, if you don't mind."

"I'm sorry. I was just wondering how I could ask you to go easy on her. She's had a pretty bad time, one way and another."

"You can stay with her if you like and see I don't try any rough stuff! All I want is a few facts."

"I've been telling her that since Friday," Amory said mildly.

"She's been with you? Where?"

"We have a cottage on the Yorkshire coast. It's very quiet. She came to me on Friday and we went down the next day. I believe over the weekend she's been able to sort a few things out in her mind. Come inside." In a relaxed and easy manner he led the way into the room off the hall which Mayo had on his previous visit assumed to be the study.

"Rachel," Amory said as he went in, "there's someone to see you. It's—"

"I heard, Josh. Hello, Mr. Mayo."

"Miss Dove."

Now that she was here in front of him he found it curiously difficult to begin. She had resumed her seat at the large mahogany desk, which was piled with papers she was stuffing into cardboard boxes, presumably for the fire. Amory perched on the corner, swinging a negligent foot, while he himself occupied the chair opposite. He had the feeling they were ranged together, maybe against him. But she smiled suddenly and said, "I owe you an apology. I shouldn't have gone away like that, but I needed time to think."

"Next time you need to," he answered austerely, not willing to forgive quite so easily, "just let me know first. In fact, while you were away thinking, we've learned quite a bit about what happened last Sunday. So now I'd like to hear the truth from you, if you please."

"Yes, of course. It wasn't very sensible not to have told you in the first place."

He didn't feel an answer to this was called for. It confirmed a long-held belief of his, that a high IQ had very little to do with everyday commonsense. Those who claimed to be intellectuals were often quite spectacularly lacking in that commodity and the ability to manage the everyday affairs of life. Amory didn't on first acquaintance seem to fall into this category. He appeared pretty down to earth, and with a leavening of humor which he didn't think Rachel possessed. She looked happier, however, and more relaxed than when he'd seen her before. He suddenly noticed that the portrait over the desk, presumably of her father, had been taken down. He wasn't surprised. He imagined it had been the first thing she'd done before sitting at the desk. How her father had managed to sit under the cold regard of his own flat brown eyes, the mouth closed like a trap, perhaps to disguise its weakness, was unanswerable. His daughter didn't have to.

He collected himself and began to take her through the events of Sunday, starting with her arrival at the lockhouse and her departure back to her university. Amory was able to confirm the time of her arrival. He lived in college and it appeared she had gone straight to his rooms. Her account of what had happened at the lockhouse tallied in every respect with what Steven Cordingley had said.

"You saw them quarrelling and yet you were quite happy to leave her alone with him?"

"It had blown over by the time we left. I think he was genuinely sorry that he'd upset her and he was being especially nice to her. He's really quite charming when he wants to be."

Mayo hadn't found him charming at all, but he allowed that women looked at things in a different way. "And after you left the Jubilee?"

"I drove straight back up north, dropping Ken and Shirley at the Wainwrights on the way. That was the reason we'd gone in my car, Ken's very sensible about not driving after he's been drinking, and someone else at the dinner party had previously agreed to give them a lift home."

One more thing he wanted to know. "When we spoke before, you told me the reason your mother asked to see you was to tell you about her illness."

"That's right, it was."

"And that was all?" She didn't answer. "Wasn't it about Steven she wanted to talk as well? Or did you know about him before then?"

She flushed and looked unhappily at Amory for support. What she saw there Mayo couldn't tell, but she said, "No. Actually, neither Shirley nor I had ever heard of him until then. We'd neither of us any idea. It was quite a shock when she asked us to meet him that evening."

He thought that quite an understatement, too. It must have been traumatic to say the least, even for Rachel, but in particular for Shirley Dainty.

"So she told you Steven Cordingley was her illegitimate

grandson. I imagine she also told you who his grandfather had been?''

"Why should you imagine that? Why should she give away a secret she'd kept all her life?''

She knew, and she was lying because she also knew the father was still alive.

"It's Crytch,'' said Kite when Mayo told him what had happened the next morning. "It has to be. Farrar's already found out he was stationed in North Wales at the time, so he could easily have been our unknown soldier, home on leave. We haven't got that far yet, but it'll be him.''

Mayo nodded approval of Farrar's efforts. He was damned annoying sometimes, with his know-all airs, but he had the makings of a good copper. Give him a job like this and he'd keep his nose to the ground like a bloodhound.

"I don't want to steal his thunder, let him carry on because we shall need confirmation, but it'll cut a corner if you and I go and see Crytch personally at his office. And I want you to tell me again exactly what young Valerie said to you when she ran after you in the car-park at Dove's.'' Kite had an excellent memory and was able to repeat the conversation word for word. "We've got our man, Martin! But before we go and get him, get yourself a coffee. You might need fortifying while you listen to me and see if you can pick holes in what I say. I don't want there to be any cock-up at this juncture.''

Chapter twenty-one

Dull heavy weather had replaced the crisp sunny days, seeming to drain even the bright colour of the dahlias and gladioli crammed into the buckets of the flower-seller outside the Town Hall, and the last of the gaudy bedding-out schemes in the square of the new shopping precinct. The unstirring leaves on the trees in the park were now the heavy, dark green which says they've been there too long, it's time for a change. Some of them had already made the transmutation to pale gold. Today, the sky was that colour which is the absence of colour, all cloud. A flat, muted, nothing sort of a day. It might rain. A wind might get up and blow the cloud layer away. It might stay like this for days.

The Botticelli angel in the telephonists' cubicle at Dove's Glass had painted her porcelain features with a different palette. Her eyelids, lips and cheeks were a curious shade of tan and her hair, newly arranged in a stiff coxcomb, stood up straight from her head in no way nature ever intended, as though in fright at what had gone on underneath it.

"We'd like to see Mr. Dainty, please."

"Have you an appointment?" She didn't recognise Mayo. Callers were all one to her. He shook his head. "I'm sorry then," she said, "but he isn't seeing anyone."

"He'll see us." Mayo produced his warrant card and after a scared glance at their grim faces and a quick word on the internal telephone she told them that Mr. Bainbridge said he was in the furnace hall but someone had been sent along to fetch him.

"Where is this furnace hall?" Mayo asked.

"Oh, but you can't—" She hastily changed her mind and directed them along a route which involved going out again into the car-park and turning right into the yard, where they found the place easily enough. They went into the long, low, seemingly ramshackle building, and as soon as their eyes had become accustomed to the darkness saw Dainty standing in conversation with someone over by one of the glory-holes that was set into the huge domed furnace. The scene was like something out of hell, Mayo thought, the heat, the dark, the half-naked men, the swinging irons to which orange-hot gathers of molten glass were attached, swishing through the air with little apparent respect for anyone in the way. Dainty stood waiting for them to approach, his face expressionless, his hand on the back of a bench with long wooden arms where the sitter rolled a bulb of fiery glass metal on the end of a pipe. This man would be the blower, the head of the team, the gaffer, supreme in the glassworks succession, Dainty as he had once been.

It was easy to imagine Dainty at home and content here before the furnace, stripped to the waist, his torso gleaming with sweat, ox-like shoulders lifting and swinging and wielding the heavy weight of glass. Now he looked haggard, Mayo saw as they came nearer, his forehead was dewed with sweat, but that may have been merely due to the dimness of the interior and the searing heat.

"Come to look round then, have you?"

No-one could seriously believe they would take time off in the middle of a murder enquiry to be taken round the works like a Women's Institute outing, no-one could be that naive. It showed his mind had been elsewhere. It had been something said without thought, a banality uttered to cover up the awkwardness, the embarrassment of their arrival. Men were looking speculatively at them, putting two and two together.

"We'd like a word in private, Mr. Dainty, if you please."

He turned and spoke briefly to the man beside him and then motioned them to follow him. They walked in silence out through the back door of the hall, then in single file up some steep, narrow back stairs and finally into his office. The light was poor on this dull day. Automatically, Dainty crossed the dove grey carpet and pressed the switch that illuminated the corner cabinets, another that lit a single green lamp on his desk. He lowered himself into his chair like an old man, all his vitality and energy gone, a defeated Minotaur. The effect of that vibrant colour and lighting in the dim room, and the solitary man sitting with his head supported by his hand was that of an actor sitting on a stage, waiting for the curtain to go up and the play to begin.

Mayo waited for Dainty to speak first. At last he said, "What is it you want of me?"

"The truth about what happened last Sunday."

"The truth?" He looked round the room in a vague distracted way, as if that were something he'd lost and might never find again. "Well I—well." On his desk was a carafe of water with a tumbler over its neck. He poured a glassful and drank it thirstily. "Where do you want me to start?"

"After you got back from the golf club in the afternoon will do for the moment."

"We came home and read the Sunday papers, dozed in front of the telly, went out to dinner with the Wainwrights . . . you know all this, I've already told you."

"What you haven't told us is where you went after you had your snooze and before you had dinner."

"Ah," he said, then looked up with a show of his old belligerence. "If you're asking that then you must know the answer."

"You tell me, all the same—and no more funny tricks. You're already in serious trouble for wasting police time . . . you, and your wife, and your sister-in-law."

"I don't know what you mean," Dainty said, but he did. And he knew that Mayo already knew the answer. The bluster went out of him. "All right, we called in to see Marion. Who's told you, Rachel?"

Mayo shook his head, and the blood rushed to Dainty's face as further realisation struck. "All right," he said again after a minute. "Since he's obviously told you his version, I'll just put the record straight."

"We're listening."

But his account of what had happened at the lockhouse turned out not to differ substantially from that of Rachel or Cordingley. The disparity with the latter was only in the interpretation. Where Cordingley had implied treachery in Dainty's having him investigated, Dainty insisted that this had been the right and proper and only thing to do to avert total disaster within the firm. The slight disagreement Steven said he'd had with his grandmother over her refusal to come out with her plans for him Dainty implied had been a major row.

"Yet you left her alone with him?"

"By that time things had simmered down," Dainty admitted. "He'd apologized to her, and we had to go, we had a dinner date, remember? But if you think I came back and murdered her, you're mistaken. I wasn't going to have that young puppy putting his penn'orth in here at Dove's, mucking up everything I've been trying to do, I'd have fought like hell to stop it, but I didn't kill her!"

"Let me ask you something, Mr. Dainty. You obviously knew Steven Cordingley was a protege of Mrs. Dove's, but do you know who he really is?"

"I don't give a toss who he is, he could be the Prince of Wales for all I care, it won't alter my attitude! She said he was her grandson, but who the father was is anybody's guess. Somebody she had an affair with during the war, I reckon. Ships that pass in the night."

Did he really believe Marion Dove had been like that?

The thought communicated itself to Dainty. He had the grace to look ashamed, but it was himself he was really thinking of. "You have to believe me, you know! I didn't kill her—why should I be such a fool as to risk everything I've ever worked for? What I mean is, I wouldn't have killed her anyway—"

"As you say," Mayo answered. "It's good to know your heart's in the right place, Mr. Dainty. But just now I'd like to have a talk with Mr. Bainbridge, if it's all the same to you."

He came into the office, leaning heavily on his stick, but looking rather better, presumably after a weekend of rest, than Mayo would have expected. There was even some slight colour in the marble face but less rigidity in the way he moved, the way he lowered himself in silence on to the upright chair by the window, and waited for what they had to say.

Mayo began, "The last time I saw you, you told me you weren't able to help us in the matter of Mrs. Dove's murder. That was nearly a week ago. We've reason to think you might want to change your mind."

Bainbridge's eyes, over his half-moon spectacles, regarded him steadily. "Now why should you think that?"

"We've traced Steven Cordingley."

"Ah."

"We're aware of the circumstances surrounding his proposed introduction into the firm here, and the objections to it. I think you know all about that—and precisely what happened last Sunday evening. Whoever you think you're protecting, I'd advise you to think again and tell us what you know. I presume you know why we're here and you're now prepared to tell us?"

A slight, bitter smile twisted Bainbridge's pale features. His answer was bleak. "There's really no need to presume at all. I'm quite ready to tell you what happened."

It had been very dark, under the trees up by the old lock gates. He was grateful for that, and the respite. He could rest on the lock stairs, swallow one of his pills and wait stoically for the pain to assume more manageable proportions. He sat there in the shadows, the Malacca cane with the silver handle that had been his father's a support to lean against, and waited for the car parked beside the house to leave. That boy should have been gone long before now, it was getting late, time was pressing. It had taken him an hour, possibly more, he couldn't remember, to drag himself here, yard by painful yard, sliding each foot forward, hesitantly, so that if anyone had seen him, they'd have thought him a drunken man. He'd pretended to Gwennie over the week-end to be worse than he was, but now he had no need for pretence, he'd scarcely ever felt worse. But he would spoil nothing by giving in, at this stage. He was a patient man, prepared to go on waiting, and it was essential that he should remain calm for what he had to face.

The sweet, heavy scent of the honeysuckle climbing round her door pervaded the night. White phlox, starring the darkness, added its own layer of fragrance. A car's headlights scimitared the darkening road above, the noise of its engine increased as it crossed the bridge that spanned the canal, stopped and then after a while started up again. The door slammed, and then silence again, but for the gentle papery sound of the breeze ruffling the reeds.

He lost track of how long he had waited, occasionally getting up heavily and moving around with the aid of his stick so that he wouldn't stiffen up, but the dusk had deepened into dark when presently a rectangle of light showed in the lockhouse doorway, framing the figure of a man he knew to be Steven Cordingley.

The door slammed behind him and he began walking with rapid strides towards his car. He'd barely reached it when the door opened again and Marion came out, calling to him. He stopped, and after a moment, turned.

Robert could hear their voices but not what they were saying. It was like a pantomime in dumb show. Her hand was on his arm, her face lifted to him, as if pleading. He saw her open her bag and press something on to him. Bile rose in his own throat as Cordingley, after a show of reluctance, pocketed whatever it was, that Robert knew must be money. Finally, he bent his head and kissed her on the forehead. A Judas kiss! She stood and watched him until he'd disappeared up the lane, and even after he'd gone and the noise of his car engine had faded, she stayed outside in the warm dark, unafraid and unaware that anyone might be watching, walking slowly back and forth along the towpath, her head bent.

He rose and stepped out of the shadows long before she reached him, so that she might see him. He didn't want to terrify her, to make her turn and run and start their meeting off at a disadvantage. But when she first saw him, he thought that was what she was going to do. She drew in her breath, and though she stood stock still, he could sense her gathering herself to turn and flee. He spoke her name, gently.

"Robert!" Her voice was constricted with shock. "What *are* you doing here, this time of night? Where's Gwennie?"

"I'm on my own."

"Gracious, how ever did you get here?"

"I walked."

"*Walked?* My dear Robert, you must be exhausted! Come inside and sit down, I'll make you a cup of tea."

"I'd rather stay out here. I want to talk to you. It may be easier in the dark."

She was immediately on the defensive. He could barely see her face, but her voice was low and urgent and he sensed the tension emanating from her. "If it's about that business, I've already told you I don't want to talk about it. I'll make my own mind up when the time is right. I'll not be pushed into any decisions. Come on now, do let's go into the house and have that tea. I need a cup myself. Today's been absolutely exhausting."

His own tiredness had gone beyond the point of exhaustion. He had made a superhuman effort and the small strength he'd regained from his rest had drained away, but he no longer felt tired or otherwise, rather a lack of sensation, a feeling of being weightless, in limbo.

"I want to ask you to think again," he said.

Into the silence a far-off dog barked, the reeds at the foot of the lock gates stirred with the presence of some unseen animal and the leaves overhead rustled in some faint atavistic empathy. She turned and took a few slow paces along the towpath towards him, as if each one were an effort. It occurred to him that Marion—Marion, strong and indestructible and ageless, had begun to seem older recently.

"I have thought, Robert."

"And?"

"I can't do what you want."

"But you must not do the other."

There was a familiar, stubborn quality about her silence. Finally, she said, "I thought you, of all of them, would understand. I thought you'd be *glad* to welcome your own flesh and blood. Don't you see, I have to do this last thing for him—he's never had the chances that Shirley and Rachel have had."

"Then give him money, for God's sake! There's no need for you to do more. It isn't you he cares for, all he wants is money."

"That's cruel! I never thought I'd hear you being cruel!"

"I'm being realistic. Face it, Marion. He'll destroy Dove's for what he can get out of it, and others into the bargain. Look at him and see him as he is. Are you proud of what we created between us? I'm not."

She raised her right hand and struck him, right across the face, and almost lost her balance. She closed her eyes and gave a little whimper, of pain, of surprise and shame at her own action. He dropped his stick and took her by the upper arms and her eyes flew open. "Come to your senses, don't be such a *fool!* Can't you see what you're going to do to everyone, to Rachel and Shirley —most of all, to Gwennie? My God, have you even *thought* what will it do to Gwennie?"

He shook her violently and for a moment they teetered together on the edge of the canal. Part of it fell away into the water and his grip tightened, pulling her away from the edge, afraid she might go into the water. She moaned again, and as he looked at her, he could see death in her face, the stark shape of the skull beneath the tight-drawn skin. She was a gargoyle, her lips drawn back in fear, her eyes wild. But still she shook her head. He lost all sense of time, or reason, he could see nothing but a red mist in front of his eyes. His hands round her neck felt preternaturally strong, as they hadn't felt for years.

It didn't take much effort. She hardly struggled at all. She went limp and quite soon he knew she was dead.

He released his hands and she fell away from him backwards into the water. He stayed where he was, petrified as sense returned, unable to move for several minutes. Then he looked down, and saw with horror that her body hadn't sunk much below the surface, it was supported by the mud and reeds that had silted up the canal. He had no strength left to move her, to push her out into the deeper water at the centre where she would sink. With an anguished cry, he groped for his stick, then staggered, almost crawled, up the lane.

At the top, where it emerged on to the road, a girl was manoeuvring a car out through the gate of a field where it had been parked, the car he'd heard draw up earlier. She got out to lock and close the gate behind her and for a crazy moment he was tempted, almost beyond resistance, to beg a lift of her but sanity, or self-preservation, triumphed over his weakness. He thought he might well die before he reached the sanctuary of home again, and at that moment would have welcomed it. It didn't matter what happened to him now. He had done what was necessary, now Gwennie would never, ever know how he'd betrayed her.

After Bainbridge had finished speaking, no-one seemed inclined to say anything. Dainty looked like a man in shock. In the dim light, with his pale polished face, Robert Bainbridge bore an uncanny resemblance to that black and white photograph of his daughter, to Rose.

Dainty poured another tumbler of water and drank. *"You were the father of Marion's child?"* He sounded stupefied. "I don't believe it!"

"I don't suppose you do, but I wasn't always old, and a cripple." Exhaustion was evident now in the dragging way he spoke, the faint flush had intensified to two bright spots on either cheek, and his eyes were very bright. His speech had lost its pedantry, and seemed to have regained some of its former local intonation.

"I came home on leave the day after their house in Chapel Street was bombed. The place was in ruins, her mother and father had both been taken to hospital. Marion was staying with relatives." He paused but went on almost immediately. There seemed little point in trying to stop him, since he evidently had the guilty person's intention of making a clean breast, and enough of his own brand of determination to carry it through. "She used to cycle up to the hospital every evening to see her parents. I was at a loose end, so I took to going with her, for company. One time, after the visiting, we rode round the countryside a bit . . . it was a beautiful evening, it was May, the May blossom was out on the trees. Well, she'd been very brave about it all but that evening for some reason she broke down. I tried to comfort her, one thing led to another . . ."

He'd forgotten the others by now, he was speaking to himself, looking inside himself. "God alone knows what got into me —except that she was there and Gwennie wasn't—when all I wanted, all I've ever wanted, was Gwennie. Nobody could have been more shamed than I was, than I've always been." He closed his eyes and then said, tonelessly, "I didn't rape her, you know. She wasn't unwilling. And I-I wasn't the first, either."

No. There had been Geoffrey Crytch. But Crytch's unit had left Wales and had been fighting in North Africa in May 1943. That was what he'd told them an hour ago. It had been necessary to check that he couldn't have been the soldier Collis had remembered, although Mayo had been as nearly positive as ever he could be, after Mrs. Cordingley's mention of Rose's birthday, that Robert Bainbridge, on leave at the time of the bombing, the relevant time, was the father. And that, as far as Robert Bainbridge was concerned, had constituted motive enough.

"That's why, when I eventually learned about the baby," Bainbridge was doggedly going on, "I never thought it could have been mine. But I *didn't* know about it, not until long after we'd been married, Gwennie and me. I'd no reason not to believe the story about Marion having some sort of nervous trouble and going away to stay with that aunt—I'd seen how upset she'd been that night, so it didn't surprise me. It was years later Gwennie told me the truth. Neither the parents nor Marion ever mentioned it, there was this conspiracy of silence, pretending nothing had happened, nobody was supposed to breathe a word about it. So I couldn't have asked Marion herself without letting her think Gwennie had broken her promise never to speak of it. And anyway, I reckoned if she'd thought the baby was mine, she'd have told me, wouldn't she?''

It was what he wanted to believe, he had convinced himself that it was so. "Besides, we've never had children of our own, we've never been lucky that way. What a terrible thing it would have been for Gwennie to know . . .''

He leaned back in the chair and ran a finger round the inside of his collar. His knuckles were white as he leaned forward on his stick. As he must have leaned on the fateful night, waiting for Steven Cordingley to go, making indentations in the ground which might have been, but were not, the marks of high heels.

"When did you realize the child was yours?" Mayo asked.

"Not until a few weeks ago. She came to me and told me she'd always bitterly regretted having the baby adopted and finally she'd decided to do something about it and have it—the little girl she'd called Rose—traced. I begged her not to do it, to let sleeping dogs lie, but she'd made her mind up and she wouldn't listen. She said nobody need ever know that Rose had anything to do with me, she'd kept her silence all these years and she wasn't about to break it now. Well, as you know, the trail ended in Steven Cordingley.''

He broke off once more to mop his forehead. He'd been talking practically non-stop, feverishly, as if he had to get everything out as quickly as possible. "Take your time, Mr. Bainbridge," Mayo said. Bainbridge merely waved his hand impatiently and went on. Mayo didn't try to stop him. They were getting the confession they needed, which was just as well, since without it, there was precious little to prove him guilty of the crime he'd committed.

"I knew as soon as I saw him that he was trouble, in every way. Bad for the firm, but even worse for me—and Gwennie. You've seen that young man. Does he strike you as the sort to pass by the chance of finding out who his grandfather was? The first time he met me, he began asking questions. He's the sort who'd not stop until he'd ferreted the truth out. And he'd have used it, believe me!"

Mayo didn't doubt this for a minute.

"She went a little mad, I think. Now that she'd found him, there wasn't enough she could do for him, even to standing by and seeing him ruining the firm she'd given most of her life to."

"And that was important to you?"

"Yes, of course it was, in a way. But there's only one thing— one person—really important to me, who's ever mattered, and that's Gwennie. She's stood by me through thick and thin, even when I came out of the forces a crock. I couldn't, I *wouldn't,* let her know, that I'd been disloyal to her, and with her sister, her sixteen-year-old sister, how could I? What has she done that she should be made to suffer? To share my guilt? There was *nothing* I wouldn't have done to protect her from that kind of hurt."

It occurred to Mayo as he looked at the man, that here was the face of a fanatic. Men with eyes like this, burning in their sockets, the skin of the face stretched taut over the bones, had roasted at the stake for their beliefs. Men who'd achieved unbelievable feats of heroism, near miracles, by the sheer strength of their willpower, by an unswerving single-mindedness. It no longer seemed impossible, or even unlikely to believe, that Bainbridge, lame and in constant pain, had dragged himself from Holden Hill to the Jubilee Locks and then strangled a woman with his bare hands.

"But good God, to kill her!" Dainty exclaimed, appalled.

"I didn't mean to," he said, as they so often did, afterwards, "I loved her, as we all did. If she'd listened to reason, it wouldn't have happened. And I-I didn't know she was ill, dying."

"If you had, would it have made any difference?"

Bainbridge said nothing. His face was livid, he looked very ill. Then he said, bleakly, "No, very probably not."

He might not have planned to murder her, but had it been entirely an accident? He must have made his schemes for that day, a last bid to make her see sense. He had let slip that he had seen Marion the previous Friday, *after* her quarrel with her sister, he'd told Mayo how upset she was about it. She had been in the office at Dove's on the Friday afternoon and according to Valerie had seen Bainbridge as well as Dainty. Steven Cordingley was certain she had cancelled her usual Sunday lunch arrangement. Not with her sister, however, but obviously through Bainbridge. He hadn't told Gwen, because that would have involved explaining about Steven. Presumably, he had hoped to persuade Marion to think again and they could have found some way of accounting for her absence.

That was how Mayo and Kite had thought it must have happened. Mayo turned to ask Bainbridge, but he was speaking again, his voice sounding strange and slurred. "It's very warm in here, a glass of water—"

Dainty blinked like a man coming out of hypnosis and picked up the half-empty carafe on his desk. "I'll get a clean glass."

"Never mind that, use the one that's there," Mayo ordered, springing to the old man's side. With equal alacrity, Kite leapt to fill the tumbler and Mayo said to Bainbridge, loosening his collar, "Have you any pills?"

A faint shake of the head. The flush had gone, the face was a pallid grey, like cold porridge, but his mouth twisted into a parody of his old, ironic smile.

"None left," he said.

He wasn't going to need them, anyway. Not now.

Chapter twenty-two

He'd rarely felt less inclined to meet and talk over the events of
a case with anyone. At the lockhouse, what was more, a rendez-
vous he liked no better. But Mrs. Bainbridge had asked to meet
him there and he felt he owed her that, at least, so Mayo took
himself off with as good grace as he could muster.

The leaves were falling from the trees in great autumn drifts,
but the little house didn't have the forlorn, deserted air he'd
expected. It was still furnished as it had been when Marion
Dove lived there, Mrs. Bainbridge had lit a fire against the chill
and there was the everlasting pot of tea ready, and a plate of
warm, lavishly buttered scones. Then he noticed the net curtains
at the windows, the brass ornaments . . .

"You're living here," he said, taken aback and trying not to
show it.

"I couldn't stand it, up there in Harmer Street, not without—
not on my own, but I'd nowhere else to go until I thought of
this. I like it here anyway, and I've got Paul living with me. He
has a makeshift bed on the sofa for now, but we've got other
plans. I'm going to have an extension built on with a room
behind he can have for his own. It won't be very big, but I don't
suppose he'll be with me for long, they want to be off on their
own these days. I shall miss him, he's been such a comfort. But
by the time I get the extension finished, they'll have opened up
the canal and what I thought was, I'd start up a little tea-room,
for people on the boats. What d'you think of that?"

At first thought, the whole idea seemed macabre and ghoulish
in the extreme, planning to live here where such a horrific tragedy had occurred, involving the two people she had loved best.
But perhaps it wasn't. Maybe, by not shutting it out of her mind,
she'd more easily be able to come to terms with what had hap-

pened, find the same sort of peace her sister had found, be able to "kiss the joy as it flies."

In the last weeks she'd put on weight. She was evidently one of those who ate for comfort, not one who dwindled away to nothing through grief. Her hair was white at the roots where the tint was growing out, and if she was pale, her make-up concealed it. She was as smartly dressed as ever, and the black suited her. He felt like clapping, or perhaps weeping.

When he'd eaten as many scones as he could manage—he was taking Alex out to supper tonight—and manfully drunk two cups of tea, she poured herself a third cup with plenty of sugar, then settled back in her chair and fell silent. The logs on the fire threw sparks up the chimney. Suddenly she said, her voice not quite steady, "He did it for me, you know. He did it all for me, and there was no need. That's what upsets me. No need for any of it, because I knew."

Once more she'd succeeded in astonishing him. "You knew?"

For a moment the lines of communication were crossed. Then she saw what he meant. "I'm not talking about Marion dying, though that's all part of it, of course. I meant I'm the one who's to blame for all this. I ought to have told him, but I didn't have the courage."

"What did you ought to have told him, Mrs. Bainbridge?"

"That I knew about the baby. I've always known it was his, see. Well, not always, but soon enough. The more she refused to talk about it, the more it made me think. I started putting two and two together and well . . . once I'd faced the possibility, everything else fell into place. I'd nothing to prove I was right, but there's times when you don't need proof, when you just know. I wasn't jealous or anything, I knew there'd couldn't ever have been anything serious—and anyway, he was married to *me*, it was *me* he loved. Always."

"You can't blame yourself," he told her, but couldn't quite bring himself to add what he also felt, that Bainbridge should have been the one to tell her the truth. Of all people, surely he could have trusted Gwen to understand. Not allowing her to forgive indicated a kind of arrogance.

"As to the other—I didn't know he was responsible for—for her dying, not at first, how could I? It was only when you started asking questions about the baby that I began to be frightened it

might be that. But I put it to the back of my mind, I refused to
admit it could be possible. I wouldn't think about it. The other
felt worse, somehow, him finding out that I knew about the
baby. It was something I'd dreaded happening for years. He'd
never have been able to bear it, you know.''

Their eyes met. She knew why her husband had done what he
had done. It was probable, if hard to credit, that Bainbridge had
acted as he did simply to protect his wife. So hard that Mayo
would never wholly countenance it. In part, it must have been
true, and Bainbridge himself had undoubtedly believed it, but
motives are seldom so selfless, or unmixed. Gwen Bainbridge
too, he saw now, had her doubts. She and Bainbridge between
them had created this image of the perfect marriage, the perfect
husband, and she alone knew that it had not been in his nature
to admit to her he had, even once, had feet of clay.

So this was why she had asked him to come here. She'd realized too late that if the subject had been broached early in their
marriage, such a situation would never have arisen, her sister's
death would never have happened, but this was looking at
events with tragic hindsight. It wasn't his job to reassure her, to
tell her what she needed to be told, that she had done the only
thing possible in the circumstances. Probably there was no-one
else she could talk to, no-one who knew all the facts. He did his
best. They talked for a long time. But he didn't think she'd ever
be totally convinced.

He came out of the overheated cottage and stood at the foot
of the first lock for a moment or two before walking up the lane
to his car. The tall plants by the water's edge had a black, shriv-
elled look, the water was no longer green but dark and oily,
brambles that the devil had spit on caught at his trouser legs as
he turned to leave. He wouldn't come here again. He walked
up the rutted lane to where he'd parked his car at the top, and
then drove back to Alex.